D1616003

Wound Tight

STRIPPED DOWN (novella)
WRAPPED AND STRAPPED
HANG TOUGH
TRIPPED OUT (novella)
RACKED AND STACKED
WOUND TIGHT (novella)
SPUN OUT (AUGUST 2019)

Want You Series – Contemporary Romance
I WANT YOU BACK (APRIL 2019)

Mastered Series – Erotic Romance
BOUND
UNWOUND
SCHOOLED (digital only novella)
UNRAVELED
CAGED

Need You Series – Contemporary Romance
WHAT YOU NEED
JUST WHAT I NEEDED
ALL YOU NEED
WHEN I NEED YOU

Single Title Novels
RUNNING WITH THE DEVIL – Erotic Suspense
DIRTY DEEDS – Contemporary Romance

Wild West Boys Series – Contemporary Romance
MISTRESS CHRISTMAS (novella)
MISS FIRECRACKER (novella)

Single Title Novellas
LOST IN YOU (short novella) – Contemporary Romance
WICKED GARDEN – Erotic Romance
BALLROOM BLITZ – Contemporary Romance

Mystery Novels Written As Lori Armstrong

Julie Collins Series – Private Eye Mystery
BLOOD TIES
HALLOWED GROUND
SHALLOW GRAVE
SNOW BLIND
DEAD FLOWERS (novella)
BAITED (novella)

Mercy Gunderson Series –Mystery/Thriller
NO MERCY
MERCY KILL
MERCILESS
DOUBLE SHOT OF MERCY – Short Stories coming fall 2018

Wound Tight

A Rough Riders/Blacktop Cowboys® Crossover

By Lorelei James

1001 Dark Nights

EVIL EYE

CONCEPTS

Wound Tight
A Rough Riders/Blacktop Cowboys® Crossover
By Lorelei James

1001 Dark Nights
Copyright 2018 LJLA, LLC
ISBN: 978-1-948050-31-9

Foreword: Copyright 2014 M. J. Rose
Published by Evil Eye Concepts, Incorporated

Acknowledgments from the Author

This book is dedicated to my BFF/PA/Cheerleader for team LJ and author whisperer, Kim O'Connor – Happy Birthday!! (and I'm not dedicating this to you just because I haven't sent your birthday gift yet). There'd be no love story for Callie and Justin if not for your brainstorming help last year when you said…whatever happened to Justin Donohue? Doesn't he deserve a happily-ever-after? Add in Callie Morgan, a much younger, very feisty character we last saw at age four, and BOOM—this May-December romance was born. Thank you, Kim, not just for helping me with this idea, but for the love and support you give me personally and professionally every single day. I hope I never have to do without it…XOXO

To the always fabulous, amazing, stupendous Liz Berry – thanks for your patience and friendship during what's been a rough year for me. Your generosity continues to astound me and I'm still blown away that I get to call you a friend and that I'm a beach babe for life!

To the 1001 Dark Nights/Evil Eye team—MJ Rose, Kim G., Jillian Stein—another one in the books! Happy to be part of this amazing project!

Sign up for the 1001 Dark Nights Newsletter
and be entered to win a Tiffany Key necklace.

There's a contest every month!

Go to www.1001DarkNights.com to subscribe.

As a bonus, all subscribers will receive a free copy of
Discovery Bundle Three
Featuring stories by
Sidney Bristol, Darcy Burke, T. Gephart
Stacey Kennedy, Adriana Locke
JB Salsbury, and Erika Wilde

One Thousand and One Dark Nights

Once upon a time, in the future…

*I was a student fascinated with stories and learning.
I studied philosophy, poetry, history, the occult, and
the art and science of love and magic. I had a vast
library at my father's home and collected thousands
of volumes of fantastic tales.*

*I learned all about ancient races and bygone
times. About myths and legends and dreams of all
people through the millennium. And the more I read
the stronger my imagination grew until I discovered
that I was able to travel into the stories… to actually
become part of them.*

*I wish I could say that I listened to my teacher
and respected my gift, as I ought to have. If I had, I
would not be telling you this tale now.
But I was foolhardy and confused, showing off
with bravery.*

*One afternoon, curious about the myth of the
Arabian Nights, I traveled back to ancient Persia to
see for myself if it was true that every day Shahryar
(Persian: شهريار, "king") married a new virgin, and then
sent yesterday's wife to be beheaded. It was written
and I had read, that by the time he met Scheherazade,
the vizier's daughter, he'd killed one thousand
women.*

Something went wrong with my efforts. I arrived in the midst of the story and somehow exchanged places with Scheherazade – a phenomena that had never occurred before and that still to this day, I cannot explain.

Now I am trapped in that ancient past. I have taken on Scheherazade's life and the only way I can protect myself and stay alive is to do what she did to protect herself and stay alive.

Every night the King calls for me and listens as I spin tales. And when the evening ends and dawn breaks, I stop at a point that leaves him breathless and yearning for more. And so the King spares my life for one more day, so that he might hear the rest of my dark tale.

As soon as I finish a story... I begin a new one... like the one that you, dear reader, have before you now.

Prologue

From that first deep thrust, Justin Donohue knew he was a goner.

A goner.

Totally gone for this girl.

If he kept going…he'd never want to leave the tight, wet heat of her body.

That's what she wants. She'll get her hooks in you and never let go.

The warning *too soon, too young* got louder and louder, drowning out everything else.

A burning sensation squeezed his lungs, expanding until he feared it'd tear him apart.

I can't breathe. Why the fuck can't I breathe?

Then he made the mistake of looking into Callie's eyes.

Something more than lust shone back at him.

Hope.

He blinked, trying to erase the expression he'd seen on her face, praying he'd misread it.

But at second glance, it hadn't changed.

It'd intensified.

Not that. Give me any look but that one. I'm not the man you think I am.

"Justin," she said softly. "Don't."

"I can't do this."

"Wait—"

But he didn't. He pulled out of her abruptly and scrambled off the bed.

Immediately the heat and urgency that had driven him to this point morphed into a cold sweat and he started to shake.

He found his clothes and dressed quickly, silently begging her to let him escape without discussing what a spectacular fuck-up this was.

It doesn't have to be. You can fix it.

Don't second-guess yourself. Just go.

When he heard her inhale, he braced himself.

"You're leaving?"

Justin gave her a curt nod and reached for his hat.

"Fucking me was that much of a disappointment?" she demanded.

"One thrust isn't fucking, Callie."

"What we were doing before that one *non*-fucking thrust…doesn't count?"

Justin lifted his chin. "All of it counts—"

"Don't say it," she warned.

"—as one big mistake," he finished.

"You don't mean that."

He didn't know what the fuck he meant. Or what he wanted…except to get out of here so he could breathe. So he could think. Maybe then he could silence the voices warring inside his head.

"I'm sorry."

She didn't say one word in return.

Yell at me, call me names because you know how to get to me.

Talk about sending himself mixed messages. He couldn't stay, but he didn't want to go.

Fear won out over hope. It always did for him.

His boots barely touched the floor as he ran out.

Chapter One

Three days earlier…

"Have you seen the new ranch hand?" Callie gushed to her coworker Svetlana.

Svetlana—aka Lana—took a break from mopping and looked at Callie. "I cannot keep up with all of the new hires," she said with a sniff.

"Oh, come on. How could you have missed him? I swear his hotness even made Mrs. Gradsky blush—and she's been surrounded by good-lookin' cowboys her whole life."

"Did our boss lady catch you drooling over this man?"

"God no. I was literally hiding in the bushes outside the office as I picked up trash." Callie sighed. "I had to stay still even when I wanted to break the damn branches to get a better look at that killer ass of his."

"You were checking out his…?"

Her mind supplied "package" but virgin Lana would blush ten shades of crimson if Callie admitted that. Instead she said, "Behind? Of course. Such a hardship, watching that perfect cowboy butt sauntering away from me. But he did me a solid before he disappeared inside the office. He turned around and his frontside was just as delicious as his backside." She whistled. "The man has it going *on*. Dark blond hair, vivid green eyes, great smile." Amazing smile. Even from thirty feet away the man oozed charisma.

"You are what my mama used to call boy crazy," Lana said.

"I'm not interested in boys. I'm interested in men." Not that a man like him would take interest in her, especially not when she was covered in dust after a full day of doing grunt work.

"You are certain this new ranch hand is not married?" Lana asked.

"I assume not since he's living in the bunkhouse with the rest of the hired hands."

"How do you know that?"

Because curiosity had gotten the better of her. Despite Lana's claims there were too many new hires, there actually weren't. The Gradskys paid their employees very well, so employee turnover at the rodeo school or the ranch associated with the school was nearly nonexistent. When a new school session started there was an influx of students and parents, but the local staff only increased by two or three. And in the year she'd worked there, none of the hires had looked like him.

"Cal-lee," Lana accused, stretching out her name. "You followed him."

"I noticed him and another guy hauling some stuff from the parking lot into the bunkhouse." She frowned. "He didn't have much, now that I think about it."

"Probably because he got kicked out of wherever he was living before. If he's that good looking the guy's probably a major player." Her eyes took on a mean glint. "I hope if he cheated on his wife she took him for everything and he has to start over with nothing."

Lana assumed the worst about everyone—men especially. Which made zero sense since she'd never had a boyfriend.

"You know Annie will set her sights on him, so get ready for some competition."

"If Miss Wantscock hopes to try her luck with him, she'd better do it fast because I'm calling dibs, right here and now."

Lana rolled her eyes. "One day you'll slip up and call her Wantscock to her face instead of her actual last name."

"If my last name was *Hadcock* I'd have a great sense of humor about it," she retorted.

"Then you should be laughing when Dickie calls you 'the Morgan fair child.'"

"I laughed the first fifty times. Then he forgot my first name is Callie and my last name is Morgan. For about two weeks I had to ask people to stop calling me by my last name."

"Is there anything else I need to do before I head into town for my bartending shift?"

Lana pointed to the two bags of trash by the door. "Drop those in the dumpster on your way to your camper."

"No problem. Are we scheduled together tomorrow?" As much as she liked working with Lana, she wasn't crazy about janitorial jobs. She'd much rather be outside.

"I don't know. Mrs. G will give us our assignments after the staff meeting tomorrow morning, so don't forget about that."

"I won't. Thanks. See ya."

Callie exited the classroom building and crossed the parking lot to dump the garbage. Then she took the path that zigzagged through the massive Grade A Rodeo Academy compound until she reached the employees' campground.

There was room for ten RVs, but only two spots were currently filled. Since the rodeo school rotated different teachers into the curriculum, many of them opted to live in a motor home for the nine-week course. Callie had chosen the spot closest to the road so she wouldn't disturb the others when she pulled in from her bartending job at three o'clock in the morning.

Although she was just a temporary resident, she'd arranged pots of flowers around her camp spot to create a homier appearance and added a chair and a small table under the pop-out awning. She stopped and fussed with pots of petunias that looked droopy. Hopefully she'd get free time to fertilize her plants and wash the exterior this weekend.

Callie unlocked the door, cleared the steps, and breathed a happy sigh. Her home was her haven and she rarely invited anyone into it. Bill, the maintenance guy, was the only person she worked with at Grade A who'd been inside her domain, and that was only because she'd asked him to check out why her air conditioner wasn't working. None of her fellow "Foxes"—the nickname given to The Sly Fox Saloon bar staff— had been issued an invite. After living in, and frequently being evicted from rental trailers growing up, she wanted her own place...a place no one could take away from her.

She'd purchased the older model fifth wheel at an auction for two thousand bucks, which had emptied her piggy bank of nineteen years' worth of savings. There weren't major issues with any of the camper's electrical, mechanical, or plumbing systems, but the interior had been destroyed. She'd salvaged what she could and spent every free moment of the next year making it livable—painting the cabinetry, installing new flooring, reupholstering the cushions. Then she'd scoured secondhand stores for furniture, rugs, curtains, blinds, and dishes. All items she'd chosen reflected her style in a way she'd never been able to express, and she'd finally felt like an adult. An adult who was more than ready to leave the nest and fly away.

Callie glanced at her phone to check the time as she unplugged it from the charger. Most days she left her phone at home. Chances were high it'd fall out of her pocket when she was mucking stalls and a horse or a cow would step on it. The Gradskys kept her busy and she didn't have time to mess around on social media apps during working hours anyway, much to her younger twin sisters' dismay that she rarely Snapchatted with them.

She ate a sandwich while she loaded up her gym bag with her outfit for the night. The only stipulation for her "uniform" at the bar was it had to be sexy. After grabbing an apple, she shouldered her bag and locked up. Then she hopped in her truck and headed to town to finish the last eight hours of her sixteen-hour workday.

* * * *

On the half-hour drive, Callie called her family. Chelsea was at soccer camp and couldn't talk. Cameo's number immediately kicked over to voice mail—who knew what that wild child was up to. She connected with her mom briefly, catching her before she started the second half of her split shift at Lucky's Tavern.

Callie had done her time at Lucky's. And at Big Red's before that. And the Rail Station before that. The Morgan women—well, at least she and her mom—were pro shift workers in bars. They'd lived hand to mouth even before Callie's dad died the year she'd turned eight. After that, they'd moved from place to place, barely one step ahead of eviction notices, child services visits, and bill collectors.

But they'd survived.

Before Callie moved away from home last year, she'd promised her mother that she'd never work as a stripper. Her mom wasn't a judgmental woman, but that demand had come from out of nowhere. That's when her mom had told her about her younger cousin, who'd taken a "temporary" job as a stripper, gotten mixed up with a motorcycle club, and literally turned into a crack whore who died at age twenty-one.

The same age Callie had been when she left home.

No stripping had been an easy promise to make.

But Callie recognized the parallels between The Sly Fox Saloon and a strip club. Sixty percent of the clientele were men, and the female waitstaff danced on the bartops for extra tips. Even the employees' area in the backroom was set up with makeup stations complete with Hollywood lighting and boasted a separate section with a mirrored wall positioned above a wooden floor where the servers could practice their dance routines. The only differences between this bar and a gentleman's club were the staff served drinks in risqué clothing versus no clothing—they were still using sex to sell booze and entertain. Callie had no problem with that.

"Omigod, Calamity, I'm so glad you're here!" Vivi cried out. "Look at my hair! I can't do anything with it." She caught Callie's eye in the mirror and batted her fake eyelashes. "Please help me."

"Of course. Lemme get dressed first."

Callie dropped her bag on the end of the bench. Off went the flipflops, jeans, T-shirt and bra. She slipped on a tiny pair of cutoff jean shorts, the frayed edges barely covering her ass. The white lace push-up bra amplified her already ample cleavage. Over that she wore a skintight white camisole with a deep V-cut dotted with rhinestones. A sleeveless red and blue plaid western shirt left unbuttoned and red cowgirl boots with two-inch heels finished her ensemble.

Neenah, the oldest Fox at age thirty-two, gave Callie a shoulder bump as she passed by. "Girl, I hate that you threw on that outfit in under a minute and you look amazing." Her gaze traveled down the front of Callie's body. "Take advantage of those long, shapely legs and perky tits while you can, Calamity. Find you a man now, 'cause it all starts to go south after thirty."

"Hah! More like it starts going south after twenty-five," Vivi retorted.

"Oh, shut it, you two," Callie said grabbing a wide-toothed comb. "You both are freakin' gorgeous. And I don't need a man to take care of me. I do just fine taking care of myself."

"Wouldn't it be a relief to have someone to share the burden with?"

"What burden?"

"Life."

"If your life is a burden, then you're living it wrong." She moved in behind Vivi's chair. "What look we aiming for tonight?"

"Jailbait. School girl uniform." Vivi smirked. "That short of a skirt definitely would've gotten me kicked out of St. Mary's."

"Private school? Wow, Vivi, your family must've been rich." Callie had to drop out of school at sixteen when her mom got laid up for three months and couldn't work.

"Rich. Right. I'm one of nine kids. School uniforms meant my folks didn't have to buy us clothes." She sighed. "Would you have time to jazz up my makeup too?"

Callie pointed at her own face. "This needs work first since bare-face ain't an option here like in my other life. If there's time left over, then I'll fix..." Callie peered at Vivi's eye makeup. "Christ, did you use that magenta eye pencil *again* after I told you not to?"

"But I love it," Vivi said with a pout.

"But Vivi, it doesn't love you. That hue is not in your color wheel, as I've told you half a dozen times. It clashes with your auburn hair and eyebrows."

"Listen to her, Vivi," Mandy said from the chair next to hers. "Our Calamity knows her shit when it comes to beauty. She's going pro with it, remember?"

Going pro. Callie looked over her shoulder and said, "Ssh. Not so loud."

"I didn't realize it was a secret," Mandy said in a low voice.

"It is...and it isn't. You know how the Barbarian is about us voicing ambitions beyond shaking our tits and ass for cash. I can't afford to lose this job when I still have to earn a shit ton between now and registration deadline or I'll have to sit out another year."

Vivi and Mandy mimed zipping their lips.

Neenah patted her shoulder. "You're gonna be a superstar and we can all say we knew you when."

Callie lowered her head to hide her eyes. She loved these women. They supported her in ways even her family hadn't. Ever since the first time she'd cut her doll's hair and pilfered her mom's makeup, Callie had dreamed of working in a salon. It'd taken her longer to get to this point than she'd planned, but now that goal was finally within reach.

Loud clapping alerted them to the presence of Barb—aka the Barbarian—the front end manager. "Foxes. Listen up. Men's night means we'll be busy early, so I wanna see your asses on the bar dancing every thirty minutes. If your section is slow...you know the drill. Three-minute solo dance. Any questions?"

No one spoke.

Barb scrutinized each of the seven servers all dolled up...and then

Callie. She lifted an eyebrow. "You're on in ten minutes, Calamity. Get your makeup finished and your hair did and quit helping everyone else."

"Yes, ma'am." She twisted the ponytail holder around Vivi's thick hair and pulled it tightly, fanning it out. "Done. Now move your ass so I can get ready."

Vivi kissed her cheek and whispered "Thanks" as she passed by.

With no time to do pigtail braids, Callie fluffed up her honey-brown/reddish gold hair—a custom dye she'd formulated herself—with a shit ton of hairspray. She totally rocked the trailer park beauty queen style tonight. She finished her face in seven minutes with time left to dust shimmering powder on her chest, arms, and legs.

Callie remained behind the bar for the first two hours of her shift since she was a fast pour bartender and happy hour was always crazy.

During the first lull, something compelled her to glance at the entrance.

Her heart thundered when she saw the hot new ranch hand she'd spied on at Grade A.

The man could stop a damn cattle stampede looking like that. Black hat, fitted white western shirt, jeans, boots and the commanding presence that sucked the oxygen from her lungs and probably the air from the entire bar.

It'd been ages since she'd felt that twist of immediate lust.

Was he a player? Would he treat every woman to that panty-melting smile? Or would he act cool and aloof? Like he knew he was *all that* and he could have his pick of anyone in this bar.

The guy he was with—the other new hired hand—said something and the object of her lust laughed.

Sexy smile and a deep, unselfconscious laugh?

Yes, please. She wanted to feel that laughter against her throat. As she rode him to sweaty, loud orgasmic bliss.

At least four times.

She continued to watch him as he ambled toward the bar, that sexy-as-fuck cowboy saunter speaking volumes about how well he moved.

Well, buddy, I've got moves of my own.

He hadn't noticed her yet and it was high time to change that.

Callie waved to the DJ. Then she hoisted herself onto the bar and did one slow spin around the pole to the whoops and hollers of the men surrounding her as she waited for the music signaling her solo dance to start.

Chapter Two

"I can't believe you dragged me to a titty bar," Justin Donohue said under his breath.

His new coworker Deke smirked and paid the cover charge.

Justin dug cash out of his front pocket and handed it to the beefy brunette bouncer manning the door. She smiled at him and said, "ID too."

"Are you serious?"

"Company policy for anyone under thirty."

Was this woman screwing with him? He hadn't seen "under thirty" in a damn decade. He handed her his Colorado driver's license.

Her eyebrows disappeared into her hairline when she saw his birthdate. "Wow. Great genes, cowboy." She gave him a pointed once-over from the tips of his boots to his belt buckle. "You look great in those jeans too. Come find me later. I'll save you a special dance."

I just bet you will.

He followed Deke into the main part of the bar. They stopped just inside the door.

"See? This ain't a titty bar," Deke said. "They've got their clothes on." His gaze tracked a statuesque blonde wearing a leather corset and white lace skirt, sheer enough to see her red thong. "Mostly."

Justin laughed at that. This Deke kid was a character. "Not a titty bar, but damn close. You brought me here the first day we met. I'll be interested to see how you top that on day two."

Deke grinned. "I figure we'll be too tired tomorrow after the first official day of work to do anything but sleep."

"I hear ya. Come on. I promised I'd buy the first round." Justin headed toward the bar. A few "excuse me's" and the crowd of mostly men parted.

That's when he saw her.

And they had the "our eyes met across a crowded room" moment that he'd dismissed as pure hogwash when he'd heard it from other guys.

But it was as real and as breath-stealing as a 1500 pound bull tossing him to the ground.

His wet dream cowgirl broke eye contact, jumped up on the bartop, and took a couple of spins around the pole. Then she nestled her spine against the metal, propped one booted foot up behind her and bowed her head in a classic cowgirl pose.

The guys watching her whistled and stomped their feet, waiting for the music to start.

Still buzzed by their simple eye fuck, Justin racked his brain, trying to guess what song she'd picked to torment him and every other man in the bar.

"Legs" by ZZ Top?

Nah. But damn…those legs deserved their very own song.

"Dead or Alive" by Bon Jovi?

Doubtful, even when it had a western flair.

"Man, I Feel Like A Woman" by Shania Twain?

Nope, not that one either.

"Save A Horse (Ride A Cowboy)" by Big and Rich?

Too obvious. He had the feeling she wouldn't pick an ordinary or clichéd song. Definitely no "Pour Some Sugar On Me" by Def Leppard or "Redneck Woman" by Gretchen Wilson.

The first few notes were lost to the crowd, but he watched as her boot on the pole started tapping. Then the acoustic riff began and he knew he'd been right about her unconventional choice.

"Finish What Ya Started" by Van Halen.

The brazen sexpot had chosen subtly sexy.

Interesting.

The instant she started to move, Justin's heart raced.

She made swinging her hips an art form, giving everyone a sideways view of her stepping forward and back. Stopping in perfect synch when Sammy Hagar growled. Performing a little hop-skip move when the guitar plucked the high notes.

Holy fuck, she was mesmerizing.

And the meat of the song hadn't even kicked in yet.

When his fantasy woman gave the bar her back, Justin's mouth went utterly dry. Jesus Christ, she had an ass on her. Perfectly heart-shaped. Given the fact she wore short-shorts, he was treated to a peek of the sweet curves where those killer legs morphed into a killer ass. As she rocked her hips, he was damn near jealous of the faded fringe that brushed the backs of her thighs over and over.

She jumped, widening her stance, and bent forward so she was looking at the crowd upside down from between those amazing legs.

Scratch that—she was looking directly at *him* from between those amazing legs.

His dick did more than stir—the fucker stood up and saluted.

It'd been years since he'd gotten a woody in public—so long ago he barely remembered being young, dumb, and full of come.

Hell, he couldn't remember the last time he'd gotten hard and horny just from watching a woman shake what God, genetics, or a plastic surgeon had given her.

That's when he should've walked away.

But he didn't.

Sweat snaked down his spine before the babe on the bar spun around, gifting him with the view of the front side of her body.

Justin tightened his jaw to keep drool from spilling out of his mouth at his first glimpse of her lush tits.

Took him a few moments to tear his gaze away from the enticing sway of her breasts to watch how sensuously she rocked her lower half. He swore her tank top was so sheer that he could see the outline of her belly button through the clingy material.

For a split second, he imagined curling his hands around her hips as he brushed his lips across her belly, feeling her soft flesh rippling beneath his hot breath as he dragged his mouth lower and lower.

A loud stomp of her boots on the bartop jarred him from that fantasy and he refocused on her face this time. A crazy feeling of anticipation took wing in his chest when he saw her devilish smile and the challenge in her big blue eyes directed at him.

She performed a whole-body shimmy as she twisted down to a crouching position, then she twisted back up, whipping her head side to side, sending her long flowing locks—not golden blonde or honey brown or fiery red, but a fascinating mix of all three colors—swinging in an arc that never masked her angelic face.

Angelic? Nope. Any woman who could manipulate her body like that knew her way around the type of dirty that'd put a smile on the devil's face.

It definitely put a smile on Justin's.

She'd reached the section of the song where Sammy's voice had taken on a pleading tone. Keeping their gazes locked, she crooked her finger at him and mouthed the words "Now come on baby…please?"

Next to him, Deke said, "Holy fuck, man. Did you see…"

Whatever else he'd said got lost when Justin walked away from him toward her. By the time he reached her, she'd lowered to her knees. Her full lips were tilted into a sexy, secretive smile when she deftly plucked his black Stetson off his head and plopped it onto her own. Then in an impressive acrobatic maneuver, she rolled back onto her bootheels and jumped to a standing position. She spun around, shaking that fantastic ass, winking at him over her shoulder, trying to appear coy from beneath the brim of his hat.

Coy. She managed to pull off that look but he preferred her naughty do-me-baby stare.

His hard-on agreed with him.

She did the hop-skip move again, ending the song how she'd started it; relaxing against the pole.

Whistles and applause were deafening after her dance. Money that appeared on the bartop quickly disappeared as the other bartenders shoved the bills she'd earned into a white bucket.

After hopping down, she grabbed a bottled water and sashayed toward him.

His heart beat so hard and fast she likely heard it. Add in the butterflies flapping in his belly, the dry mouth, the sheen of sweat on his brow, and the painful press of his cock against his zipper, and it'd be a fucking miracle if he could even talk to her at all.

"Thanks for playing along…?" She paused and he realized she was asking for his name.

He cleared his throat. "Justin."

"Justin," she repeated with a silken coo. She passed over his hat. "Definitely a western name."

His gaze zoomed to the nametag above her left breast. "Back atcha…Calamity." He looked into her big baby blues. "Is that really your name, sweetness?"

"It's what my daddy called me."

Probably she couldn't share her real name so he didn't push. Instead, he plunked his hat back on his head and leaned closer. "Are you?"

"Am I what?"

"A calamity?"

"Depends on the day. Can I buy you a drink, cowboy hottie?"

"Why'd you wanna know my name if you aren't gonna use it?"

Calamity gave him a cheeky smile. "Because I like cowboy hottie much better. It suits that handsome face and banging body you've got goin' on."

Been a long time since Justin had blushed. He just hoped it was too damn dark in here for her to see it.

"What'll it be? You see anything you like?"

You. I'm dying to have those mile-long legs wrapped around my waist or my neck as you moan my name.

Her eyes widened as if she'd read his mind. "How about we start with one drink and go from there?"

"Cool. Coors. In a bottle."

"Coming right up."

As soon as she was gone, Deke appeared at his side. "Man. Are you a chick magnet or what? It looked like she wanted to jump off the stage and start bouncing on your pole."

"She just needed my hat as a prop for her dance."

Deke raised his eyebrows. "Plenty of dudes in cowboy hats here." He pointed at his own head. "Including me. So it's gotta be you."

Justin shrugged.

"While you're getting up close and personal with her, don't forget you're the DD tonight."

"You planning on getting hammered, boy?"

"Nope. But I ain't about to take a chance drivin' even if I only have three beers tonight." Deke tossed him the keys. "Don't ditch me neither. Even Uber ain't gonna drive that far out."

"No worries." Justin watched the swing of Calamity's hips as she approached. "I've got a reason to stick around."

Calamity handed him the beer, which he passed to Deke. "First round is on me."

"Thanks, man."

When Justin looked at Calamity, she'd leaned across the bar. "Did you just give away your complimentary beer?"

"Yep."

"You just cheap? Or broke?"

"Both." He offered her a charming wink. "But mostly I passed it on because I'm the DD, so I'll take a Coke."

She flashed him that dimpled smile. "One Coke coming up."

After she served him, she had other customers lined up, giving him the perfect excuse to watch her—although he pretended not to. She was an excellent bartender, pouring taps, mixing drinks, popping tops in an economy of movement that proved she'd been doing this job long enough to be comfortable with it.

While Calamity was friendly and joked around with customers, her interaction with them never veered into false flattery territory just to score a big tip—unlike some of the other servers he noticed who all but gave their customers lap dances.

He watched the redhead sporting the Britney Spears schoolgirl outfit working the back of the room, flirting and hustling for every dollar. But the men she waited on lapped up her attention like eager, frolicking puppies, meaning it was mutually beneficial—who was he to judge?

"Your face is gonna freeze like that if you keep scowling," she said behind him.

"Sorry. Habit." He turned around.

Those huge blue eyes studied his face. "Why is it a habit? Is your life really that bad?"

Might be clichéd since she was a bartender, but he didn't hesitate to confide a partial truth. "Not bad, no. Just...unsettled."

"Woman troubles?"

"Only woman I see that might be trouble for me is you, Calamity."

"Charmer," she groused. "That sounds promising. But tell me more about you feeling unsettled."

"I started a new job today."

"Ah. So you're not from around here?"

"Nope."

She smirked at him as she fixed a cocktail in a tall glass. "Should my next question be 'what's your sign?'"

"Maybe my sign is 'out of order' or 'needs replacement parts' or—"

"Don't feed the bear," she supplied.

He laughed. "You're funny, Calamity."

"I try." The redhead caught her attention and she nodded. Then she focused on him. "Laugh at my jokes, cowboy hottie, but please don't laugh at my dancing."

"Laugh? Why would I do that? I've seen you dance, remember? And, darlin', that ain't something I'm likely to forget anytime soon."

She blushed. "Not this one. I hate it, but it's a crowd pleaser."

A bartender at the opposite end of the bar rang the cowbell on the wall and all the servers jumped up on the bartop.

"Cotton-eyed Joe" began to play and the ladies did a line dance, hopping and skipping and twirling. Then they did a fake kissing thing that was sorta cheesy.

But throughout the performance, Justin kept his eyes on Calamity. Her body language gave no indication that she disliked giving the performance. She smiled and clapped as if she was having the time of her life.

His first thought? All women were damn good actresses when they wanted something.

His second thought? When the fuck had he turned into a cynical, grumpy old man?

You've been that way for longer than you wanna admit, Donohue.

Money littered the bar after the song ended.

Then Calamity was back doing her job without missing a beat.

After she served the last customer in her line, she returned to him. "You're still here."

Was it his imagination or did she sound pleased about that? He jerked his head to where Deke sat with a couple of women. "My buddy ain't eager to leave."

"Are you?"

Justin locked his gaze to hers. "Nope. Unless I'm bothering you? Keeping you from doin' your work?"

"God no. It's already slowed down. And the floor manager can't bitch at me for doing what I'm supposed to."

"And what's that?"

"Personally interacting with customers." She angled closer. "To be honest, cowboy hottie, I haven't *wanted* to personally interact with any customers."

"You mean recently?"

"No, I mean ever."

Don't be a grumpy old man and call bullshit on that. "Is there a rule against getting friendly with customers after hours?"

She shrugged. "I've had no reason to ask management or the other servers..."

Until now went unsaid.

"How long have you worked here?"

"Over a year."

"How long you been bartending?"

"Six years."

Justin did the math. She had to be twenty-one to serve alcohol...add six years...so she was twenty-seven at the very least, although she looked younger than that.

Dude, you're forty. At twenty-seven she'd still be too young for you, the angel on his right side reminded him.

She's more than old enough, the devil on his left side retorted.

"Which side is winning?" she said softly.

"Pardon?"

"Which side is winning?" she repeated. "The part of you that's attracted to me? Or the part of you that wants to ask me a million more questions before you make an informed decision on whether you'll personally interact with me?"

How had she homed in on his internal war so quickly? His eyes narrowed.

Calamity laughed. "I'm very good at reading people, Justin. Very good. That's why I'm choosy about who I interact with."

"And what's your bead on me?"

She scooted in closer, so close he got a whiff of her hair, and goddamn if that fruity, perfumed scent didn't zoom straight to his groin.

"You're a loner. But you haven't always been that way. I'll bet you were a fixture in a bar like this a few years back. You and your buddies probably had contests to see who could pick up a chick the fastest and get laid the fastest." Her eyes roved over his face, her heated gaze stopped on his mouth and she spoke to his lips. "No doubt with your gorgeous mug and muscled body you usually won those bets—I imagine you arguing with your friends that getting blown in the bathroom of a honky-tonk *does* count as sex, since you've proved many times that nearly any woman you smile at is eager to drop to her knees for you."

Holy. Shit. He started to speak, but she shook her head.

"Huh-uh. I'm not done. But those days are behind you. Your buddies have settled down with families and you're still living the wild life. Yet...despite you being in a bar tonight, I'm guessing you don't troll for pussy anymore...not that you ever had to work *that* hard for it. These days you're the 'one and done' guy, but even that isn't as frequent as it used to be. You've closed yourself off—maybe you're disillusioned because your career has stalled, or maybe you're sensitive about being the black sheep of your family, or maybe some stupid woman ripped out your heart and it still fucking stings that you trusted her with it. Or maybe..." Her blue-eyed gaze hooked his again. "Maybe you won't let a woman get close because you don't want her to see the real unsettled you beneath the charming, carefree cowboy persona."

Justin said nothing.

Calamity didn't smirk like she'd won some kind of game. All she said was, "By the scowl on your face, I hit it dead on, didn't I?"

Tell her she's wrong.

But she wasn't wrong...not entirely. Not that he intended to point out what part of that little pop-psychology she'd gotten right.

"Well, sweetness, since you seem to think you've nailed me good and hard"—he flashed her a devilish smile—"now you gotta give me something sweet and true about you to soothe my ragged soul."

She rolled her eyes and said, "You can beg better than that."

Christ, he liked her spunk. "What makes you think *I* ever have to beg for anything?"

"I bet you don't so maybe it's past time that you learned," she shot back.

"All right." He angled across the bar and placed his mouth on her ear. "I have no problem begging for what I want when it's just you and me, baby. I'll even get on my knees for you."

Her breath hitched.

"Words ain't my strong suit. But I promise you that my mouth is better suited for more creative, nonverbal ways to beg." He paused, letting his warm breath flow across her ear and down her neck. "How'd I do?"

He heard her swallow hard. "Winner, winner, chicken dinner. What do you want?"

"For starters? Your real name." He moved back only far enough to gaze into her eyes. "Whisper it to me in that sexy bedroom voice you've been taunting me with."

Her dazzling smile about knocked him sideways. "It's Callie."

Almost without thought, Justin tucked a hank of her silky hair behind her ear. "Thank you, Callie."

"Now that you know it, what will you do with it?"

"Use it when I beg for your phone number."

"And if I say no?"

He smiled. "I'll keep begging until you say yes."

"Normally, I like that relentless quality in my men. But you've got my name, cowboy, and that's more than I've given anyone else. Let's call that a win for tonight."

"Calamity. Girl, what's a man gotta do to get a beer?" a man complained at the end of the bar.

She retreated and sent the customer an exasperated look. "Wait your turn, Jimbo."

"How come he gets a longer turn than everyone else?" He shot Justin a glare. "It's not fair."

"Life ain't fair. And he's a damn sight prettier to look at than you."

Jimbo scratched his beer gut as he studied Justin. Then he shrugged. "You got a point. You'd better make my G&T a double to take the sting outta that comment."

She laughed and the sweet, dirty sound went straight to Justin's dick.

He and this woman could have some serious fun together.

Justin hung around, hoping for more…conversation or interaction, or he'd even take them making fuck-me eyes at each other, but Callie didn't look his way again for half an hour. He'd even gone to another station to get a refill on his soda.

When business didn't slow, he said fuck it and tracked down Deke. Besides, Justin hadn't come into town to get laid. If he wanted more of her, he knew where to find her.

Given Deke's bleary-eyed reaction to Justin calling his name, it was past time to go.

Deke's new lady friends booed loudly as Justin herded him out the door.

"Christ, man. I shouldn't have had that last shot of tequila."

"At least if you barf it'll be in your own truck."

Deke snorted and climbed in the passenger side.

Justin had his hand on the door handle when he heard, "Justin. Wait."

Turning, he watched Callie hustle across the parking lot. Goddamn she was something. Legs, tits, eyes, hair—every inch of her screamed hot sex.

Fuck, he wanted some of that.

Bad.

"Hey. Sorry I didn't get back to you in there."

He shrugged like it hadn't been a big deal.

And she called him on it. "Don't do that."

"What?"

"Dismiss me."

"Sweetness, you don't owe me nothin' and vice versa. It was nice meetin' you and passing the time."

Her full pink lips parted—not quite a jaw drop, but close. "Seriously? That's what you think I was doing? Passing the time?"

"Weren't you?" Then he pushed her just a little more. "You admitted you were supposed to interact with the customers. Helps increase your tips, don't it?"

"Except you didn't tip me, cheapskate."

Do not be an ass and ask if that's why she chased you down.

But she seemed to read his mind anyway.

Her eyes flared with anger and then her expression changed to pure deviousness.

Ah, fuck. He was in for it now.

"And you didn't get this either," she said huskily as she slipped her fingers under the strap of her camisole, over the swell of her left breast and into the cup of her bra.

Justin hoped anger would cause her to root around recklessly and her nipple would pop out. *Please, be angry for just one more moment.* Holding his breath, his eyes locked onto every tug and ripple of fabric…it seemed to be taking her a long time to find whatever she'd shoved in there.

A soft moan drifted to him.

Christ, was she stroking herself? Right in front of him?

He managed to tear his gaze away and meet her eyes. "Not nice."

"Neither were you."

"I can play very nice." He started toward her. "In fact, I'll help you find whatever you lost in your cleavage."

She backed up. "That's downright hospitable of you, cowboy hottie."

Justin grinned and kept up with her retreat, step by step. "Why you tryin' to get away from me?"

"Because we both know how this is gonna end."

"You don't want that?"

Her gaze dropped to his mouth. "I shouldn't."

"But you do."

That's when she stopped moving, allowing him to catch her.

"So do I. Jesus, I want a taste of you like you wouldn't fucking believe."

Placing his left hand in the center of her chest, he slowly moved it up until his thumb could feather across the spot in her throat where her pulse raced.

Her breathing was hard and fast, yet she stayed perfectly still.

Content to let him lead? Another plus in her favor. Then he cupped the back of her neck, holding her in place as he brought his lips to hers.

Heat, lust, and her sweet scent swamped him.

Justin wanted to devour her.

And he ached to savor her.

Callie angled her head, familiar enough with kissing a cowboy to maneuver around his hat. She parted her lips beneath his, her tongue licking the underside of his teeth in a surprisingly erotic way.

When he groaned his appreciation, she thrust her tongue into his mouth and kissed the hell out of him.

Why had he deluded himself that she'd just hand him the reins?

The woman knew what she wanted and she took it.

Christ, that was hot.

She fisted her hand in his shirt and held on.

Justin clamped his other hand on her ass and shifted them a quarter turn, so anyone coming out of the bar wouldn't see Calamity in a lip-lock with him. This kiss was nobody's business but theirs.

He could've stayed right there, all night, just kissing her.

But someone—that drunken ass Deke probably—laid on the horn, and she broke the kiss.

Staring at him, she fought for breath. Then she said, "I knew you'd kiss like that."

"Like what?"

"Like every kiss would be different with you, every time. But you'd know exactly what kind of kiss I'd need."

Justin didn't even know what the hell to say to that.

Callie pulled a folded piece of paper out of her bra and held it up.

"What's that?"

"My number." She sauntered forward and tucked the paper into the front right pocket of his jeans, casually letting her fingertips brush his shaft. "And you didn't even have to beg," she whispered against his mouth, nipping at his bottom lip before she retreated. "See you later, cowboy hottie."

Chapter Three

Callie dragged herself into arena one the next morning, taking her seat next to Lana as stealthily as possible, ignoring her friend pointedly tapping on her watch.

Yeah, yeah, she was ten minutes late. Didn't appear that she'd missed much.

Chuck and Berlin Gradsky, hands-on owners of Grade A Rodeo Academy, stood on the arena floor in the dirt in front of the twenty-plus staff members.

The hierarchy of employees was reflected in the seating assignments. The rodeo school instructors were parked in the front row. Behind them were the stock handlers. The third row was filled with kitchen staff. And the last row—Callie's row—were the groundskeepers and maintenance crew.

The stock handlers usually sent one guy to represent them. Not today. Today six black-hatted heads were present. But with all the guys wearing the required uniform of black cowboy hats and white shirts, Callie wasn't sure which one might be Justin. Maybe as the newest hire, also known as the lowest man on the totem pole, this meeting wasn't mandatory for him.

She could hope. She had no idea what she'd even say to him now.

"Students start arriving late next week," Berlin Gradsky continued. "We'll have a welcome banquet to kick things off the first night."

Members of the kitchen staff asked questions about the menu, which annoyed everyone else. So Callie tuned out.

God. She was tired. Napville beckoned—four hours of sleep wasn't nearly enough. She'd started to drift off when Lana elbowed her.

Berlin was still talking. "This is a young class and several parents will be staying over to serve as chaperones."

Dickie asked, "The bunk houses will be full. Where's everyone stayin'?"

Another question that had nothing to do with her.

Her stomach growled and she and Lana both giggled.

Berlin's gaze scanned the group until it landed on her. "Just a heads up, Callie, that you won't be tending bar much over the next nine weeks."

A head whipped around so fast the hat on top of it nearly flew off.

Well, at least now she knew where Justin was sitting.

She kept her focus on Berlin, and her voice steady. "You'll give me a list of the students who can have a toddy or two?"

Berlin smiled. "You got it."

Callie finally allowed her eyes to meet Justin's.

Poor man had a shit poker face.

Anger warred with disbelief and his scowl indicated anger was winning.

She fluttered her fingers at him in a friendly wave.

Her attempt at levity didn't soften the hard line of his jaw.

At all.

Lana knocked her knee into Callie's and whispered, "OMG. *That's* the new ranch hand?"

"Uh-huh."

"Okay, so he is all that, but he also looks a little mean."

"He's pissed off at me."

"Why?"

"We…interacted last night at The Sly Fox and I didn't mention that I worked here. Then again, he was too busy staring at my tits to share his job title either, so I figure we're even."

"Interacted?" She lowered her voice. "Did you do it with him?"

Do it. Callie snickered at virgin Lana's phrasing. "No, but we kissed the hell out of each other."

Lana had no response for that.

Chuck Gradsky took the microphone from his wife. "As most of you know, we rotate instructors at the rodeo school. But this session, with one exception, we've gotten the same poor suckers to sign on again we had last session."

Laughter.

"Melissa Grant is teaching cutting horse and penning classes."

Melissa waved her hand.

"Jerry O'Dell, two-time world CRA champ in saddle bronc, is back on board."

He waved his hat above his head.

"Sharla Hodges, the owner of eight—count 'em eight—CRA world championships in barrel racing, is in charge of that program."

Sharla lifted a metal crutch up in acknowledgment.

"On the bareback side of things, we've got Ryan Desanto, who's competed in the CRA world finals three times. He'll be here next week."

"Team ropin' will be taught by Cres and Wyn Grant. No world championships, but they've been ranching and ropin' together their whole lives and know the meaning of teamwork."

Callie leaned in to whisper to Lana, "Why is Chuck telling us about the Grant brothers' qualifications? We already know this."

"Maybe it's for the benefit of the new ranch hands? Or maybe he's practicing the introductions since he has to do it again with the students next week."

That made sense.

"Breck Christianson, three-time winner of the All-Around title in the CRA, has taken on the responsibilities of teaching bulldoggin' and tie-down ropin'. Usually Breck also teaches bull riding, but this session, we're thrilled that he's got an assistant coach. Please welcome the newest member to the Grade A Rodeo school, Breck's fellow South Dakotan and professional bull rider and world champ, Justin Donohue."

Callie froze.

What the actual fuck?

Justin…her Justin…was a Professional Bull Riders champion?

Didn't see that one coming, did you?

Seemed she wasn't the only one who'd left out a few pertinent details last night.

But she'd followed the PBR for years and his name wasn't one she remembered. Which meant he was a lot older than he looked.

When Justin tried to get away with just waving his hat, Chuck said, "Newcomers have to stand up."

Justin stood, smiled, and waved.

None of his friendliness was directed at her.

Lana murmured, "I thought he was just a ranch hand?"

"Me too."

She pulled her phone out of her back pocket and typed JUSTIN DONOHUE in the Google search engine. She zoomed over to the Wiki page and in less than thirty seconds had answers to her questions.

Name: Justin David Donohue
Hometown: Faulkton, South Dakota
Age: 40

Holy shit. She'd been sucking face with a forty-year-old guy?

That's why he was so damn good at kissing. And flirting. A guy that age, who looked like him, probably fucked like a dream too.

Giving a mental shrug, she kept reading.

Marital status: Single.
Children: None.
Championships: Two world, two iron cowboy competitions, twenty-seven individual events.

It listed a span of two years where he hadn't competed. Due to an injury? He'd staged his comeback with a vengeance because after the break was when he'd started winning.

So Justin had competed in the PBR for twelve years and retired from the sport five years ago. There wasn't any mention of what he'd been doing in his retirement. Why resurface now to take a position as an assistant instructor and a lowly ranch hand?

Because he's just another cowboy, riding the coattails of his former rodeo glory, with nothing to show for his years on the blacktop except a couple of championship belt buckles, a battered body, and a beat-to-shit pickup. Now he's relegated to flitting from place to place doing odd jobs, living off the generosity of his friends and former colleagues.

Sounds cynical, Calliope Jane Morgan.

No, that sounded like her dad.

Her dad had retired after a serious rodeo injury. Then, because he couldn't stand living a normal life with his wife and three daughters, he went back on the road to reclaim his glory, and went beyond being just dead broke—to just plain dead.

Nope, she wasn't bitter about that at all.

"And last, but not least," Chuck Gradsky said, interrupting her brooding, "this here is Deke. Our newest hired hand. Stand up, son."

Deke stood and doffed his hat, bowing as deeply as a dandy in a Shakespearean play.

Lana gasped and blurted out "Dibs" so loud that Deke heard her.

He grinned, winked at her, and bowed again.

"Now I believe you about that lust at first sight thing," Lana said dreamily.

"Mess around with him, but don't fall for him," Callie warned. "Transient guys like him will leave your heart broken and your bank account empty when they skip town."

Lana blinked at her. "But…"

"Trust me on this, okay?"

"Okay." Lana continued to stare at her.

"What?"

"Will you be taking your own advice with the bull rider?"

There was a loaded question.

"Any other questions?" Chuck asked them pointedly.

Callie saw Annie raising her hand.

Lana and Callie exchanged a "here we go again" look.

"Yes, Annie?"

"As head chef, I'll need to visit with the new employees privately about their dietary restrictions."

"Think *Wantscock* will share her dietary restrictions of being a *maneater* with the new stock handlers?" Lana said snarkily.

Callie pretended to knuckle away a tear. "I'm proud you're bringing out the claws to fight for your new man crush."

Lana blushed.

After Chuck dismissed them, Callie was the first one out of her seat.

She barely made it outside the arena before she felt a strong hand on her shoulder.

Then she was face-to-face with one annoyed cowboy.

Maybe not…face-to-face since he towered over her by eight inches.

Damn, the man was gorgeous even when he was annoyed.

"Is there a reason you're running away from me, Calamity?"

Despite the rapid fire of her pulse, she managed to act unaffected. "Ego much, champ? Or maybe I should say, ego much, Mr. Two Time PBR World Champ?"

Justin's lips flattened. "Answer the question."

"I'm not running from you. Staff meetings eat up time and I've got a shit ton to do today before I go to my other job."

"Why didn't you tell me last night that you worked here?"

"Same question back atcha," she retorted. "When you said *I started a new job* you could've mentioned where you were literally hanging your cowboy hat, but you didn't. If you had…." She shrugged.

He had no response for that.

"Look. Let's just do our jobs and we can talk later."

"I've got time. We'll talk now."

"I'm blaming you if Chuck or Berlin trot over here and chew my ass for fucking around on company time."

"How did you know that I've won two world championships? Chuck only mentioned one."

Callie rolled her eyes. Then she held up her phone. "A little thing called Google. Ever heard of it?"

He actually growled at her.

Man, she was hard up. That growl and scowl combo did it for her in a bad way.

"I know all sorts of things about you, courtesy of the internet."

"Don't believe everything you read. I guarantee most of that shit is dead wrong."

"Yeah?" She crossed her arms over her chest. "You retired five years ago. Whatcha been doin' all that time? You build yourself a nice house on a big acreage in South Dakota?"

"No."

"Have you been running your own bull riding academy? Or coaching high school rodeo teams? Or working the circuit as a rough stock judge?"

"No."

"Huh." She cocked her head. "Your bio indicated that you're not populating the world with little Donohues, so you haven't become a devoted family man. And I doubt you've become a man of God, preaching about the evils of fornication because I know firsthand how good you are with that dirty-talking mouth of yours."

"Are you always this blunt?"

"Pretty much. So let's cut to the chase."

"By all means."

"I liked you enough last night to give you my phone number."

"And?"

"And…I still like you despite all the stuff I figured out from the internet."

"Despite? I told you—"

"Ah-ah-ah. I'm talking." Callie dropped her arms, shuffling close enough to get a whiff of the starch in his shirt. "I like you despite the fact that everything you own fits in the back of your pickup, which means you're here for a good time, a short time and then you're gone." She set her hand on his chest. "Here's the truth. Guys like you are the perfect storm for me."

She laughed at his disbelieving look.

"I sound too good to be true, don't I? You're here, I'm here, we've got a wicked chemistry, why not hang out and see what happens? I promise I won't get dick-whipped—"

"Dick-whipped?" he repeated with confusion.

"Where I become obsessed with your cock."

"Sweet Jesus."

Callie laughed again. "Lighten up. This could be fun, Justin."

"Callie—"

She put her finger over his mouth. "Sexy fun times. No strings. And I promise I won't tie myself to the bumper of your truck when you leave. Just think about it, okay?"

Chapter Four

Justin suspected watching that sassy ass as she walked away might be the high point of his day.

Scratch that. Callie giving him the green light for no-strings-attached sex…might be the highlight of his damn year.

After Callie disappeared around the corner, Breck Christianson's voice boomed behind him.

"Hey, JD, there you are."

JD. Only his former rodeo buddies called him that. He faced Breck. "Now that you're technically my boss, am I supposed to call you Mr. Christianson?"

He snorted. "Hell no. And I'm not your boss. I don't know why Chuck didn't just tell everyone that you're the bull riding coach and I'm your assistant because I don't have time to do it all."

"Chuck doesn't ever do or say anything without thinking it through."

"True." He paused. "You got settled into the bunkhouse okay?"

"Yeah."

"You ready for this?"

"Ask me next week when the dorms are full of rowdy teenagers."

Breck sighed. "Sorry. That part of this sucks."

"Given my transient lifestyle, I oughta be used to it, huh?" He backtracked. Wouldn't want to oversell it. "I'll admit that the bunkhouse at the Gradskys' south ranch is much nicer. Private rooms and bathrooms."

"That's in the works for the next expansion. But Chuck and Berlin didn't expect the school would take off like it has. They only built four permanent cabins and seniority decides who gets them. With four married couples and no turnover or divorces in their respective departments…"

"I get it. Single guy, bottom of the totem pole," he joked.

"I'd offer you my motor home—that's what I lived in the first session until I moved in with Cres—but we still use it when we get free time." He paused. "I could ask around and see if anyone else has a camper to lend you."

The offer surprised Justin.

Breck's eyes narrowed. "What?"

"Honestly? The Breck I knew wouldn't have given a damn if I lived in a cardboard box if me bein' here would make things easier on him."

"Yeah. Well, that Breck don't exist anymore."

"Good. He was an asshole."

Breck laughed.

"Look, I'm sorry you went through all that shit with the CRA. I figured too much time had passed for me to reach out when I finally heard what'd happened. It wasn't like I was homophobic or I didn't want to be associated with you. After I left the PBR, I took low-key to a new level. After bein' in the spotlight, I just wanted to be anonymous and isolated for a while, you know?"

"Yeah, man. I know exactly what you mean. I did the same thing myself. But I appreciate you sayin' that, JD."

"As long as we're bein' all sappy and shit, I'm happy that you're living the life you never thought you could."

"Took me a long time to get to that point."

"Gives me hope I might get there myself someday."

"Who'da thought an alpha asshole like me who hid his preference for dick behind a reputation as a womanizer, a boozer, and a brawler, would have the happily ever before you, Mr. Clean Cut All-American Rule Follower?"

"Rule follower? Piss off."

Breck laughed. "Just fucking with you."

"I know. I make my own rules. I follow my own path. There's freedom in not knowin' what's next for me."

"You ever get tired of the gypsy life?"

Like you wouldn't believe. But that wasn't an answer anyone expected from him, so he just shrugged.

"Maybe this rodeo coach thing will work out for you and you'll like bein' in one place," Breck offered.

"It worked out for you. Cres seems like a good guy."

Breck's face lit up. "He's the best."

"You better be talkin' about me," Cres said, moving in beside Breck.

"We were. I was tellin' my fellow South Dakota farmboy that you ain't bad...for a rancher."

"Neither one of us has been a farmboy for a long damn time."

"True dat."

"We'll have you over for supper at our place some night," Cres said. "You can tell me all about my old man's high school rodeo glory days."

"That'll be a short conversation, since I won the bull riding championship every year, ain't that right, Christianson?" Justin said smugly.

"Yeah, but who won the all-around title every year?" Breck shot back.

"You...by the skin of your damn teeth."

"A win's a win." Breck draped his arm over Cres's shoulders. "Do we know anyone who's got a camper they're not usin'? Justin is a little long in the tooth to be crashing in the dorms."

Justin raised an eyebrow. "Long in the tooth? Buddy, we're the same age."

"I know. But this hot young thing makes me forget I hit the big 4-0 this year."

Cres blushed and elbowed Breck in the ribs.

"Hey, here's an idea. Have you met Callie?" Breck asked.

There was a loaded question. "Briefly."

"She's livin' at the employee campground in her fifth wheel. Maybe she knows someone. You should swing by and talk to her."

"Maybe I will."

"Cool. Let's get the business stuff outta the way."

* * * *

Three hours later, Justin flopped on the single bed in his room and closed his eyes, exhausted.

Not physically exhausted since he hadn't done a damn thing except walk and talk today, but mentally exhausted.

His whole "I'm just a broken-down cowboy, thanks for this

opportunity" bit had started to wear on him.

Because it wasn't true.

And yet some days he couldn't separate the truth from the lie—acting as if his life had morphed into a sad-sack country song, no woman, no job, nothing but an old pickup and a couple of championship belt buckles to show for his forty years of hard living.

He wasn't a dumb guy. He knew women were drawn to men who could provide for them. Where the disconnect happened was his assumption that security + money = love.

Love didn't have fuck-all to do with it. Money was everything. Without it…he was nothing to them. So the busted-up cowboy persona had started out as an experiment after his last serious girlfriend had dumped him because he hadn't learned his lesson the first time.

The first woman he believed he'd spend his life with had ended their relationship shortly after he'd taken a break from bull riding following his father's sudden passing. She loved the envious looks from other women because she'd been fucking one of the top bull riders in the world. When that ride had ended, she informed him the perks of being with him were why she'd stuck around and she had no intention of becoming a farmer's wife.

That'd ripped at him like a motherfucker.

He'd wallowed. Indulged in a few meaningless flings. Told himself he was working the wildness out of his system so when the right woman came along, he'd be ready to settle down. After dealing with his family issues, he rejoined the PBR tour and was top of the leaderboards for three years.

The next time he'd felt that pull of wanting a real relationship, he'd taken things slow and his girl seemed genuinely happy just to be with him. After luring him into a false sense of love, she'd started complaining that running with his crowd created high expectations—so she'd "treated" herself to luxuries, supposedly to make him proud to have her on his arm. The expensive things she adorned herself with were meant to show him that she appreciated his hard work and to show the world how much he adored her.

Justin hadn't given a damn about stuff. He'd wanted to build a life with her, a home, a family. Somehow she'd convinced him that if buying her stuff made *her* happy…then didn't it ultimately make *him* happy in the end too? Fucked-up logic, but he'd fallen for it. He'd wanted to believe she loved him more than his bank account…but when he'd merely curtailed his generosity with her, she loaded up the stuff he'd given her, called him a selfish, manipulative asshole and left him alone, questioning everything.

That's when Justin walked away from a life that made him miserable.

Rumors circulated in the Dallas society he'd fought tooth and nail to be a part of that he'd lost everything in a bad business deal and that's why he'd disappeared.

He didn't confirm or deny. And he realized even his so-called friends chose to believe the worst about him rather than the best.

Only one person knew the irony of the situation...that he'd quadrupled his personal wealth...and that was his older brother Jack.

Jack was brilliant, especially when it came to money. When Justin started making a name for himself on the PBR circuit and earning more money than he'd ever seen, subsequently spending it almost faster than he could make it, his big brother had a come-to-Jesus meeting. But Jack hadn't preached. Jack taught him how to manage his money. After a couple of years, the two brothers who'd been as different as night and day could spend hours on the phone discussing investment strategies.

After his relationship fiascos and his supposed fall from grace, Justin felt free. He sold his toys and his house, keeping only his apartment in Denver. He spoiled his mom, taking her on fun, spontaneous vacations. Spending time with her filled a void in his life he'd ignored after his father had died. He'd also gotten to know his nieces and nephews—but that was a double-edged sword, as he suspected it was the closest he'd ever get to having kids of his own.

He'd wandered for the past few years. He'd helped his buddy Chase McKay, another former PBR world champ, with his camps for urban kids that allowed them to experience a week in the Wild West. He'd spent a winter in Montana working for a logging company. He'd spent a summer in Idaho working on a dude ranch. Maybe it was the ultimate selfishness, but he'd done things that interested him and along the way had bettered him.

He'd finally been ready to ditch the ramblin' cowboy persona when he crossed paths with the Gradsky family. As a favor to his brother, he'd tagged along with his sister-in-law Keely when she'd gone to check out a couple of horses at the Gradskys' ranch in southeastern Colorado. While Keely haggled with Berlin, Justin got to talking with Chuck, who mentioned they were short on workers as they'd recently expanded their business.

Which was how he wound up taking a job as a ranch hand at their south ranch last year. When Chuck asked if he'd be interested in splitting his time between working with the rough stock and the students at their new rodeo academy north of Denver, he'd packed up his few belongings from one bunkhouse and moved to the next one.

This was another short-term gig in a long line of short-term distractions. Justin hadn't lied to Callie about his restlessness. While he looked forward to testing himself as an instructor, he knew it'd test him personally to live in a dorm situation with forty-some teenaged boys for nearly three months.

Two knocks sounded on his door. He said, "Come in. It's open."

Callie stepped inside and gave him a slow once-over, cocking an eyebrow at finding him stretched out on his bed in the middle of the workday.

He fought a grin. Oh, that ruffled her pretty little feathers, seeing him slacking off his first day on the job.

"I'm here on official business. Annie sent me to fetch you so you can tell her your food allergies."

"That's easy. Tell her none."

"Tell her your own damn self," she retorted. "Doesn't look like you're too busy to head up to the kitchens."

Justin laughed. "Busy is in the eye of the beholder." He tapped his temple. "Maybe I was lesson planning."

"Maybe you were napping."

"Not that it's your business, but I ran through my entire checklist with Chuck, delegated duties to the greenhorn, met with Cody about schedule changes and did a quick stock check." He flashed her a smile. "All before the staff meeting."

Her cute little nose wrinkled. "Cody didn't want you tagging along with Deke so he only had to go over things once with the new hands?"

Justin sat up and dropped his boots to the wooden floor. "As long as you're here..." He patted the empty spot beside him. "Let's clear a few things up."

He expected her to argue. But she surprised him by saying, "I'm happy our earlier talk had my desired effect that you're at least tryin' to get me into bed" as she crossed the room and plopped down.

"First off, I'm not a new hired hand. And I don't mean because I've done the job before. I've been workin' for Chuck and Berlin at the south ranch off and on for the past year."

Callie faced him. "Why didn't Mr. G mention that in the meeting?"

"Why does that matter to you?"

"Because you shouldn't be so…nonchalant about bein' in a position of authority. It's a big deal. Don't you want the respect you deserve?"

"Respect is earned." He picked up her heavy braid and tickled the side of her neck with the end of it. "But I appreciate your concern about my virtue."

"Don't poke fun at me."

She'd turned her head away.

He dropped the braid and cupped her chin, forcing her to look at him. "I'm not. My duties aren't clearly defined yet so other employees will likely question my activities—or nonactivity—same as you have. But darlin', you oughta know I have no problem bein' in charge."

A small shudder moved through her and she closed her eyes. Then she circled her fingers around his wrist and moved his hand from her chin to her chest, flattening her palm over his knuckles.

"Callie."

"Feel that?" she whispered. "How my heart is racing? You do that to me. I don't know how I'm supposed to act around you now. Like you're my boss? Like you're my friend? Like we're…"

Justin waited five long seconds for her to finish that thought. When she didn't, he said, "Look at me."

She shook her head.

"Dammit, Callie. Look. At. Me."

When she aimed that lust-filled blue gaze at him, he was done for.

He took her mouth in a desperate need for possession.

Callie didn't hesitate to give all of herself to him, but it wasn't enough.

He hauled her onto his lap, kissing her like crazy when she locked her ankles behind him.

Her hands were in his hair.

His hands were clamped onto her ass.

Their mouths stayed fused together even as their tongues warred for supremacy.

Harsh breathing, soft grunts, deep moans surrounded them as they lost themselves in each other.

Justin didn't know who'd started to slow the kiss down first. He just knew the sweet smooches, soft brushes of their lips, and the sugar bites were as necessary as their blatant show of hunger.

Callie angled his head back by pulling his hair, immediately homing in on his neck.

He kept his eyes closed as she mapped every cord and tendon with her mouth. The vibrations of her happy little moans as she discovered all of the spots went straight to his cock.

Her intense focus on him was a fucking rush but she'd had her turn...now it was his.

Justin wrapped her braid around his palm and tugged. "Scoot back."

As soon as his lips connected with the soft skin below her collarbones, he demanded more. "Tug your shirt down. I wanna taste all of you."

"Next time you don't even have to ask."

Justin might've heard fabric tear she'd complied so fast, but he was in heaven. The heavy mounds of flesh quivered as he rubbed the scruff on his cheeks across every inch. He licked, nibbled, sucked, and kissed just the upper swells until she rocked her pelvis and tried to bite back her moans.

And he hadn't even touched her nipples yet.

He buried his face in her cleavage and forced himself to slow down.

Callie didn't ask why he'd stopped. She just tenderly stroked his head.

So many things crashed through his mind.

They worked together, which meant they'd be in close proximity for the next three months. He knew the more time he spent with her, the harder it'd be to stay away from her when the workday ended. It'd been years since he'd felt this strong connection to a woman so quickly. He had no doubt they'd be dynamite in bed together and Callie had sworn she was only interested in a fling, so that was a plus. But how was he supposed to trust his instincts with her when they'd failed him every damn time when it came to women and relationships?

"Hey. Stop thinking so hard. Or get back to what you were doing."

Chuckling at her sass, Justin kissed his way back up to her mouth.

The kiss had started to heat up again when someone pounded on his door.

They both froze, eyes locked, mouths barely a breath apart.

"JD. You in there?" Deke demanded.

"Yeah."

"Can I come in?"

Callie's eyes widened.

He mouthed "Wait" and held onto her tighter in case she tried to escape. Then Justin turned his head so he wasn't yelling in her face. "Only if you wanna see me buck-assed nekkid."

"Uh, pass. But kick it into high gear, okay? That Annie chick is ridin' my ass about you meeting with her. She's pissy that I'm the second person she's sent to track you down today."

Callie buried her laugh in his neck.

"I'll get changed and meet you up there."

"Later."

Callie scooted off his lap and adjusted her shirt, then her pants, then her hair, avoiding looking him in the eyes.

He didn't like that she was retreating.

"You okay?"

"No. I shouldn't be fucking around when I'm supposed to be working."

He pulled her in close. "Can we talk later?"

She blinked at him. "We get sidetracked when we're supposed to be talking."

Justin grinned. "I know."

"I have to work in town tonight. Maybe we can find time to talk tomorrow."

"Sure." He kept watching her eyes, fascinated by the emotions she didn't bother hiding. "What?"

"Watch yourself with Annie, okay?"

"Why? You jealous already? I'm flattered, sweetness."

She rolled her eyes. "Annie has been looking to become Mrs. Somebody since I started working here last year. After today's meeting, she'll have done her research on you, Justin."

"Meaning?"

"She's seen you so she's salivating over the fact you're a cowboy hottie. She knows you're single and living in the bunkhouse, without home and hearth to go to when your teaching gig is up. She'll see your...transient lifestyle as a challenge." She ran her fingers down the pearl-snap buttons on his shirt. "Annie's on the hunt, looking to trap you and tame you."

"I appreciate the warning, but I'm a big boy." He kissed her. "Should I be worried that you know so much about Annie because you've been secretly checkin' out her wedding ideas Pinterest board?" He kept his tone light as he feathered kisses across her lips.

Callie ducked away from his kisses and headed for the door. "God, no. In three months I finally get to start my dream life—well, my dream career anyway."

"What happens in three months?"

"I start school."

"Why wait?"

She spun around. "Because I had to live in Colorado for a year to establish residency. Once I accomplished that, I applied, got my acceptance letter and I'm waiting to hear on financial aid and housing options."

"But aren't you makin' good money as a bartender?"

Her eyes narrowed. "Yes, but I want a career, not just a job."

"What kind of school?"

"In two years I'll be a licensed cosmetologist. Maybe I'll get a wild hair—ha ha—and go for an esthetician certification too. After years in the bar business, I'll just be glad to finish my last working hour of the day before two a.m."

When he stared at her blankly, she got snippy. "Don't give me that look. I have nothin' against bartending. In fact, my mom still tends bar and that's her choice. But I want a different future. Getting out of Grand Island was the first step. Starting school is the next step and I can't freakin' wait." She offered him a sheepish smile. "Sorry. I get a little wound up talking about it. Besides, I have no interest in settling down. I'm still at the 'hang and bang' stage. I've got years before my biological clock starts ticking."

Justin wondered if he looked as confused as he felt. "How old are you?"

"Twenty-two."

Jesus Christ.

He was absolutely pole-axed.

How the hell could she only be twenty-two?

And why was this the first fucking time she'd mentioned it?

His phone buzzed on the nightstand.

Callie peered at it and winced. "It's Deke. Annie's probably holding him hostage until you show up. Since the coast is clear I'll go first. See ya."

Chapter Five

"That woman is stomping on my last nerve tonight," Callie said, plunking two bottles of beer and four shots of Jäger on Neenah's tray.

"She is in rare form."

They both briefly glanced at the Barbarian, who'd moved on from chewing ass with the bar staff to ripping into the DJ. Maybe the bouncers would be next.

"I don't know what I did to piss her off," she said, adding two cans of Red Bull and two highball glasses of ice to the tray. "I'm here on time, I do what I'm told, and I don't cause drama. Yet *I'm* the one who gets penalized when Trixie-Belle shows up late, sporting a shiner and pleading to only work the floor because she needs the money?" She slammed the cash register drawer shut and nestled the change from the fifty-dollar bill between the beer bottles. "I need the damn money too. We all do."

Neenah patted her arm. "I know. It sucks. But at least you ain't dumb enough to stay with a man who smacks you around."

Callie leaned in. "It'd happen one time and one time only. Afterward I'd cut the dude's dick off and give it to the neighbor's cat as a chew toy."

"Harsh, sister." Neenah hefted the tray up with one hand. "Not all women are as strong, brave, and determined as you. For many of them, it's not a matter of choice."

"Exactly. I had no choice," she said to Neenah's back.

And she'd have no choice but to suck it up tonight too. Accept her tips would blow since she wouldn't get even one lousy solo dance on a Friday night.

Your other tips will be shit too if you don't lose the attitude.

Callie plastered on a big old smile for the next two guys that walked up to her station. "Howdy, fellas, what's your pleasure tonight?"

The blond leaned in and leered at her cleavage. "You on the menu...Calamity?"

She forced a laugh. "Nope. But I can whip up a special margarita with your name on it, slick."

"Will you stir it with your finger so I get a little taste of your sweetness?"

Eww. Even the slimy way he said sweetness made her skin crawl.

Not in the tingly, panty-dampening way that her body reacted when Justin called her *sweetness*.

Justin.

That hot make-out session on his bed guaranteed she'd be thinking about him all day and all night. But it wasn't helping now, especially when she considered Justin had acted weird after Deke's knock had interrupted them.

She turned away to mix the drinks—shaking her ass as she shook the booze together was part of the show. Normally she'd tune everything out and focus on making one drink at a time, but she'd been distracted since the moment she'd walked in here tonight.

For her...distracted meant recklessness was right around the corner, waiting to pounce and turn into chaos.

Callie's mother had joked that rare "fuck you world" look in Callie's eyes had her counting out bail money, putting the priest on speed-dial, and hiding the guns.

Maybe those actions worked as a talisman since Callie had never been arrested, gone to confession, or shot shit up in a fit of rage. What would cure her mood was one day off. Just one. Where she could lounge naked in her bed all day, nibbling on junk food, reading trashy gossip magazines, and napping.

Or better yet...Lounging naked in her bed all day with one cowboy hottie, nibbling on his junk, reading porn for dirty ideas, and napping with him lying on top of her. Or him pumping behind her. Or him grinding into her slowly. Or him pounding into her hard enough to rattle the camper and her teeth.

Oh hell yeah. Hours of hot sweaty sex...that's what Callie really needed.

She needed Justin's experience and inventiveness between the sheets. Her relatively few sexual experiences had been straightforward—

foreplay, oral sex, sex, and then they were done. She wanted the dirty thoughts she saw dancing in Justin's eyes put into action. She wanted to strip herself bare before him and say, "Show me everything I've been missing."

"Calamity? Them drinks about done?" her customer asked behind her.

She whirled back around, pouring the frothy green liquid with a flourish. "Here you go, boys. You suck 'em down once, you'll be back for more."

"That's what *he* said," Neenah chimed in, giving the guy closest to her a hip bump. "Better move, guys. The bar dance is about to start."

They paid their bill—with a surprisingly decent tip—and motored away.

Callie glanced at the clock. "Trixie-Belle isn't on yet."

"I know. But you had that *I'm gonna dick-punch these frat boys* look, so I headed them off for you." She leaned in and kissed Callie's cheek, moving her lips to whisper, "Cowboy hottie from last night is approaching. I'll run interference with the Barbarian while you do your thang."

Her guts tied into a knot and a tickle of anticipation teased her breastbone.

Neenah stepped aside and there he was.

Justin had dressed similarly to last night except he wore a tight black shirt with his black hat. The man looked good in black.

He probably looked better in nothing at all.

Callie gave him her sunniest smile. "Fancy seeing you here, bull rider. You the DD tonight?"

"Nope. I'll take a shot of Johnnie Walker Black."

He'd picked a thirty-dollar shot. Maybe he didn't know that. "You sure you want that? Bet you can't tell the difference between it and Jack Daniels."

"Bet I can."

"Fine. That'll be thirty bucks." She cocked her head at the sign behind her that read:

NO BAR TABS FOR SHOTS—NO EXCEPTIONS!

Callie walked to the back bar and snagged the JWB from the top shelf. She set a shot glass in front of Justin and poured the amber liquid to the rim.

"Reckon that I can't complain that I didn't rate one of them fancy ass-shakin' pours when you weren't stingy with this pour."

Justin's hand was completely steady when he picked up the shot glass and knocked back half of it.

He hadn't smiled at her or done that eye-fuck thing.

Uh-oh. "You seem tense. Something wrong, cowboy?"

"Yeah, Calamity, there's something wrong. Don't you think you should've told me how young you were *before* the second goddamned time I had my tongue in your mouth in the last two days?"

She froze.

"You're twenty-two. Jesus Christ. How is that possible? You told me you'd been bartending for six years. Logic dictates you'd be twenty-seven. So why did you lie to me?"

Callie had dealt with irate customers for years and she slipped into her "bless your heart asshole" persona with practiced ease. "Lemme break it down for you, Mr. Math Fail. I started bartending when I was sixteen. Yes, sixteen. My mom's uncle owned the bar so age restrictions for family workers didn't apply to me. By the time I was nineteen and working in my third bar, no one gave my age a second thought because I'd turned into a damn good bartender and that's all they cared about."

"What in the hell was wrong with your daddy that he had no issues with you workin' in a bar that young?"

Do not smack him over the head with a 200-dollar bottle of whiskey because he automatically tried to take on a parental role with you.

She rested on the bar on her forearms, allowing his hat to shadow her face from other patrons, but ensuring he saw every spark of anger in her eyes. "You don't get to come into my place of employment and grill me about things in my past and my family that don't have a fucking thing to do with you, Donohue. That's bullshit, and you know it. So why are you really here?"

"You're twenty-two years old."

"I know how old I am. Why does that matter?"

"Because I'm eighteen years older than you."

"I can also do the math."

His eyes were troubled. "I'm old enough to be your father, Callie. Christ." After he tossed back the shot, he nudged his glass forward for more. "I'm definitely old enough to know better."

"And I'm too young to know right from wrong?" she said sharply.

"I didn't say that."

"You didn't have to. It's written all over your face." She pushed upright and refilled his glass. "The age difference between us wasn't a big deal to me. But I can see that it's a big deal to you."

"Ya think?"

"You wouldn't have kissed me twice last night and for ten solid minutes today if you'd suspected I was six years younger than the age you deemed was acceptable?"

"Big difference between twenty-seven and twenty-two."

"So you drove into town to give me the kiss-off in person? You figured by doing this in public that I wouldn't make a scene?"

He grunted—maybe that passed as communication in his forty-year-old human male world, but it wouldn't fly in hers.

"Tell me something, cowboy. What part of our age difference bothers you the most? Worrying what other people think when they see us together?"

A scowl flattened his lips. "People will assume you're my daughter."

"And?"

"And I don't wanna have to explain every damn time I take you out who you are."

She shrugged. "So don't. Tell them to mind their own fucking business."

"See?" He pointed at her, his gaze dark with guilt. "That right there just proves how young you are."

And...Callie was done. "Know what I think?"

"What?"

"You're a fucking prude, Justin Donohue."

His green-eyed gaze snapped to hers.

But she continued before he could argue. "You're most worried that people will see us together and imagine us fucking. Guess what? That's human nature. If I see a hot couple, I wonder if they're having kinky sex or better sex than me because they're both sexy as fuck. Men your age will ogle my perky tits and toned ass, but they'll be jealous that you can get up in my tight, twenty-two-year-old pussy any time you want."

He sucked in a breath.

"On the flip side, you are a hot hunk of man who sure as hell doesn't look or act like forty. And your age doesn't matter because women watch you with lust, wondering about the size of your dick and what your face looks like when you come."

"Enough. You've made your point."

"I haven't even started to make my point." She poked him in the chest. "You will listen to me, Justin, because maybe then, you'll really hear me."

The muscle in his jaw ticked but he said nothing.

"You want me. You like me. Just a few hours ago you would've been happy to hold my hand and share a meal with me in public. Now, you're looking at me like I could only ever be your dirty little secret and it's wrong for you to want me the way you do. What's changed in the past six hours? Not my age. Not yours." Her eyes searched his. "Your attitude changed. Doesn't matter how you feel about me, it matters more that society dictates you shouldn't feel that way for a twenty-two-year-old?"

"You're pushin' the wrong buttons tonight, little girl," he warned with a growl.

"Call me little girl again, and I'll turn you into a fucking soprano."

"Try it, Calamity, and I'll have you hogtied so fast you'll think twice about ever threatening my balls again."

His eyes sparked with heat. Not disgust, not remorse, but pure male sexual heat.

Callie could work with that.

She brushed her fingers across his tight jaw. "If you can't get it up for me because it'd be so wrong to be sexually attracted to me—"

"Jesus, I can get it up just fine," he said with another growl.

"Whatever. Be a pal and help me pick a dude closer to my own age that I'd be better off fucking than you."

He squeezed the shot glass with such force she feared it'd break.

Riling him up…she loved that glint in his eyes.

"How about the guy wearing the Broncos ballcap to your left?" she suggested. "He's cute."

Justin's eyes never even slightly flickered that direction. "I can pull him over here by his ear gauges if you want a closer look at his nose ring."

She bit back her smile. "How about the smart-looking ginger with the beard wearing the WOW T-shirt?"

Justin finally—finally!—granted her that *I'll rock your fucking world* grin. "Baby girl, he's a gamer. He'll be fondling his joystick all night rather than fondling you, and that makes him the dumbest dude in the room."

Her breath caught. Oh, she liked that he called her baby girl. It sounded…deliciously perverted coming from him.

"So you're telling me there's not one guy in here you'd hook me up with?"

"Oh, there's one *man*. But he's still tryin' to wrap his fool head around the nearly two-decade age difference between the two of you, so cut him a little slack, huh?"

Callie grinned at him with pure relief. "How about I give you something to think about that'll likely destroy your 'look but don't touch' mindset?"

His eyes narrowed. "Don't make me out to be a fool."

"It's not my goal to embarrass you." She kissed her fingers and pressed them to his lips. "It's my goal to make you smile, make you crazy, and make you horny."

"Mission accomplished." He removed a rolled-up bill out of his shirt pocket and tucked it so deeply into her cleavage she hadn't seen the denomination. "For the shots."

Callie signaled to the DJ and hoisted herself onto the bar.

Justin didn't budge.

Not when the Barbarian and Trixie-Belle stormed over and demanded she get down.

Not when "Cradle of Love" by Billy Idol started.

He stayed right there, watching her every strut, snap, bend, shimmy shake, and jump. When she finished the dance on the opposite end of the bar, she looked over and he was gone.

But he'd left a cocktail napkin with the words U WIN written in all caps.

No, cowboy hottie, we're both gonna be winners.

* * * *

Callie didn't get the day off from her job at Grade A, but after the "stunt" she pulled at The Sly Fox, the Barbarian removed her from the schedule for Saturday night. Callie hadn't bothered to argue; she just sucked it up and promised to be a better team player in the future.

Three more months and she'd be done with it.

With a rare night off, she'd been at loose ends. She thought about holing up and watching a movie, but she'd spent too much time indoors recently. So she enlisted Dickie, Bill, and Lana's help to set-up a bonfire.

Callie's favorite part of working at Grade A was belonging to the community of fulltime compound residents who looked out for each other. Most everyone showed up, even for a little while, to shoot the breeze.

Mitzi and Bob initiated a singalong.

Tammy and Trent, the groundskeepers, brought S'mores supplies.

Grumpy old Bill, the maintenance man, shared a jug of his homemade honey mead.

Even Chuck and Berlin had dropped by with beer.

No sign of Justin.

Callie had been having too much fun to dwell on it.

By ten p.m. the fire had dwindled and only Callie, Lana, Deke, and Jerry, the saddle bronc instructor, remained.

She'd been gazing into the orange coals, content to listen to the night sounds and Jerry regaling Deke and Lana with wild tales from his years on the road to rodeo glory. But she'd even tuned that out as her mind wandered.

"Your turn," Lana prompted, nudging Callie's boot with her own.

"Sorry I drifted for a minute. What were you talking about again?"

"Growin' up and getting bit by the rodeo bug," Deke said. "It's odd that neither you nor Lana competed but here you are, workin' at a rodeo school." He squeezed Lana's hand. "Russian girl gets a pass since rodeo ain't a thing over there, but you know your way around livestock and you've got that kickass cowgirl attitude."

She pulled the blanket tighter around her shoulders. "Aw, thanks, Deke. My mom says I was born horse crazy and 'boots' was my first word. When I was four my dad got injured during bulldogging, and my mom claims he wasn't the same afterward. Took him a few years to recover and when he was healthy enough to compete, he hit the road again." She sipped the honey mead. "He fell asleep at the wheel driving between competitions and left my mom a widow with an eight-year-old and four-year-old twins. We'd been living in Buffalo Gap, where Dad worked as a hired hand, and Mom filled in for him on the weekends he was competing, but after he died we had to move. We lived with who'd ever take us for the first year. That's the way things played out until Mom got a job bartending in Kearney. I watched my sisters when she worked and babysat other kids in the trailer court when she was home. Then Mom fell the winter I turned sixteen and broke both of her wrists, forcing us to move again. We ended up in Grand Island where Mom's uncle owned a bar. Since it was a family business, I could work there without restrictions, but I had to drop out of high school. Didn't leave any time for rodeo pursuits but I did get my GED. I stayed to help out financially until my sisters were seniors in high school. Then I moved here." She smirked at Deke. "I'll expect a fifty-fifty royalty split on any down-on-your-luck country songs you write based on my early life."

"Holy shit, Callie," Lana said. "How didn't I know any of this about you?"

She shrugged. "It's in the past. I was happy to move on and get to make my own future."

"Girl, you've gotta have bitterness toward the rodeo life that took so much away from you," Jerry said.

"Actually, I don't. My folks loved bein' on the road when my dad was winning." She fiddled with the lid of her paper cup. "But I'll admit there's a disconnect for me with people who refuse to give up the dream. I'm not talking about guys and gals who compete for fun on the weekends and hang out at the rodeo grounds with their friends. I'm talking about the ones who can't accept it's time to stop and get a real job. The true ramblin' men. Working odd jobs, saving up enough money for gas and entry fees and then they're off again, striving for that perfect ride, the shortest time, and the biggest purse." She looked at Jerry. "You know guys like that."

"Not as many of 'em as I used to," he admitted. "Hard drinkin' and hard livin' takes a toll. That and car wrecks." He froze. "Sorry, I said that without thinkin'."

"It's the truth though."

Silence stretched as the fire crackled.

"Didn't mean to be Debbie Downer," Callie said.

"You weren't. I think we're all tired." On cue, Deke and Lana stood up too.

"Gonna be an early one tomorrow, so I'll help you deal with the fire."

Justin stepped from the shadows.

Callie almost jumped out of her skin. How long had he been lurking there?

He smiled briefly at Jerry and then his eyes were locked on hers. "You guys go on. I'll hang out with Callie for a while and make sure the fire gets put out."

Chapter Six

Justin didn't speak to her until everyone was gone. "Surprised to see me?"

"I figured you'd come around...or you wouldn't."

He sat across from her. "What'd you say to me the other night? Don't be dismissive?"

"I'm not." She looked at him. "I've been the decisive one. I told you where I stand and what I want. You're the one who needed time to wrap his head around our little age difference thingy."

Little age difference thingy.

He realized she wasn't being flip. It really didn't matter to her.

"Well, sweetness, I'm surprised to see you. Don't you work at the bar on Saturday nights?"

"Don't remind me." She kicked a log, sending a shower of orange sparks shooting skyward. "I'm in the penalty box tonight."

"Why?"

"The manager is teaching me a lesson. I wasn't supposed to perform any solo dances last night."

"Dancing for me got you in trouble?"

"A, I wasn't dancing just for you." She sighed. "Okay, that was a lie, I was totally dancing for you because you pissed me off and I wanted to show off."

"You certainly did that." He paused. "Good song choice, by the way."

"It was that or 'Go Away Little Girl' but I don't have a routine worked out for that one since it's ancient."

Justin threw back his head and laughed.

When he glanced over at Callie, she wore the oddest expression. "What?"

"Do you have any idea how sexy you are, Justin Donohue?"

He sent her an arch look. "If you think I'm all that, then why in the hell are you sitting so far away from me?"

In the next breath, she wasn't.

Callie snuggled herself right into his lap and draped the blanket over both of them. Then she nestled her face against his throat and sighed.

I feel the same way, baby girl.

They were content to stay like that, not speaking, watching the fire. A sense of peace that he hadn't felt in years rolled over him.

Sometime later, Callie broke the silence. "How long were you standing in the shadows?"

"Long enough."

"So you heard everything. About my childhood."

"Yeah."

"At least I won't have to explain it twice."

He kissed the top of her head. "It's been a rough go for you for a long time."

"Most of my life. But…it wasn't that bad. I mean, I don't know a different life. My mom did the best she could. I never ever doubted she loved me and my sisters. I never doubted she wished life would've been better. Even with all the struggles, the one thing she refused to do was look for a new husband for herself and a new daddy for us. Even I knew that might've made things easier, but it might've made things worse, too. She's an attractive lady, so it wasn't like she didn't have offers." She shifted to get more comfortable. "But she swears my dad really was 'the one' for her, her soul mate, all that romantic bullshit people believe."

"You don't believe it?"

"I've never seen it, never experienced it, so I have a helluva hard time believing it exists."

Such cynicism at twenty-two. Would she feel the same way when she was his age?

"Mom was always honest with me. Probably too honest. She didn't have anyone else to talk to, so she talked to me. It bothered her that my dad was the love of her life, but the love of his life was the rodeo."

The sadness in her tone ripped at him.

She kept talking. "I remember more of him than my sisters do. But that also means I'm angrier about him dyin' and leaving us destitute."

She swallowed hard. "Mom cried over him for years. Years, Justin. So the thing of it is, I remember my mom being this warm, happy, fun person when he was alive. After he died, he took that part of her with him and I hated him for that. I still do."

Justin rested his check on the top of her head. "Aw, sweetness, I'm sorry."

"Can we talk about something else?"

"Sure."

"Tell me about your family."

Of course she'd wanna open that can of worms to see if his wounds were as deep as hers. "My older brother Jack lives in Wyoming with his wife and their four kids. My mom splits her time between Wyoming and Arizona."

"And your dad?"

"Died of a heart attack years ago when I was in my twenties."

"Do you miss him?"

"Some days. My mom misses him and that gets to me. But she's much like your mom, I doubt she'll ever remarry. She's got her grandkids, two houses, and time to travel, which is an entirely different life than when she and Dad lived on the farm. Dad worked all the time and so by default, as a farm wife, so did she."

"She didn't stay on the farm after he died?"

His thoughts returned to that cold winter night that he and Jack and his mom sat around the table in the kitchen, in shock that Marvin Donohue was really gone forever.

After the funeral, it'd been a bigger shock to find out that Marvin had borrowed so heavily against the equity in the farm to keep it afloat that the bank basically owned it.

Jack had hemorrhaged money into a losing endeavor, which went against his every instinct as a businessman. But their mom had no other place to go and she was lost in grief that they couldn't rip her away from the only home she'd known for over thirty years.

"Justin?" Callie touched the side of his face, bringing him back to the present.

He looked down at her and kissed her furrowed brow. "Sorry."

"Don't relive the past in your head. I showed you my scars. It's time to show me yours."

"Bossy brat."

She nipped his chin. "We were talking about what happened to the farm after your dad died, if your memory is failing you, old timer."

Christ. The mouth on her.

He told her about the farm being in the red and possible foreclosure. "Since Jack used his money to pay off the bank notes we were unaware of, I figured the least I could do was move home, take care of my mom and the farm."

"That's when you dropped out of the PBR for a while?"

"How'd you know about that?"

"Your Wiki page."

"I have a Wiki page?"

"Dude. Repeat after me…Google is your friend."

"Smart ass." He paused. "It's weird that someone I don't know knows enough stuff about my life to post it online."

"I'm pretty sure your page is tied to the PBR main page, that's why the information is current."

"That'd make sense." But it still made him uneasy that anyone could add things to his page at any time without his knowledge or consent.

She nudged him. "Tell me more about your farmer days. Did you wear overalls without a shirt when you were out plowing up shit on your John Deere?"

"Honestly, I don't remember. I blocked a lot of that time out." A lie. He'd hated every goddamned minute of being a farmer. "One day Mom took me aside and said she knew the truth that I didn't want to be there—that I'd never wanted to farm for a livin' despite what I'd told my dad and my brother. She confessed she didn't want to be there anymore either. But because Jack believed keepin' the farm meant the world to both of us, we couldn't tell him. We phased ourselves out of the farming business slowly to make sure that's what we both wanted. We leased the land out, Mom started to travel with some of her friends, and I got back into the bull riding circuit on the lower tier."

"What did your brother do when he found out?"

"Nothin'. I'm pretty sure we never fooled him. We kept the farm for a few more years, then we sold it."

"Was that a nice chunk of money for you?"

Warning bells went off. That was the kind of question a gold-digger asked.

The tiny part of him that remained hopeful assured him that Callie wasn't that kind of girl.

His cynicism roared back, *But she is a girl, isn't she? A girl who's had a rough life and maybe she told you her sob story because she's looking for a man to take care of her. Maybe that's why she's so insistent that the age difference doesn't bother her. And how much can you truly know about her character in only three days?*

"Sorry. Forget I asked."

He chose his words carefully. "No, it's fine. I didn't see a dime of it. There wasn't much left after Jack recouped his money. The rest went to Mom."

"Ah. Gotcha."

"Anyway, the break improved my riding. Within six months, I jumped back to the top fifty and spent the next seven years livin' my life eight seconds at a time."

"Do you miss competing?"

"I miss the rush of bein' on the back of a bull and not knowing what'll happen. I don't miss all the bullshit that went along with being a bull rider. Don't miss that at all."

"I used to follow the PBR when I lived in Nebraska. On TV, anyway. But I only got to watch it if it came on during my shift at the bar."

"Who was your favorite rider?"

"Guillherme Marchi."

Justin nodded. "Guy could ride. Good guy off the dirt too."

"It's weird to think you personally know the guys I've only ever seen on TV."

Another comment that sent those warning bells ringing again.

Her eyes lit up. "But I met a famous bull rider once. I was a flower girl at a wedding in Wyoming, some friend of my parents from a big ranching family. He was a cousin of the groom. I was like five, but I clearly remember swooning when he said I'd *done a good job throwing them petals.*"

When she was five, you were twenty-three—a year older than she is right now.

Shut it, stupid mental math. Where had that fast addition been when he'd needed it in high school?

"I still remember his name, although he was done competing by the time I got interested in the sport."

"Who was the bull rider?"

"Chase McKay."

Jesus.

"You know him?"

Justin started to tell her they'd been traveling partners on the circuit for years, but changed his mind. "Yeah. We competed at the same time. In fact, my sister-in-law Keely was a McKay before she married Jack. She and Chase are cousins." Something occurred to him. "Hey, I'll bet the wedding was for Keely's brother—"

They said "Carter" at the same time and laughed.

"Small world, ain't it?" she said.

"It's about to get smaller when I tell you that Carter McKay is Jack's best friend."

"Wow."

"Yeah."

"Were you at that wedding?"

He shook his head.

"Good."

"Why?"

"Because I don't want you looking at me now and trying to reconcile it with seeing me as a little girl in a fluffy dress."

With the hungry way she was looking at him? Not a chance in hell that was going through his head.

Callie continued to stare at him as she rubbed the tips of her fingers through the scruff on his cheeks.

"What?"

"Do we know enough of each other's backstories now that we can get naked together?"

Justin turned his head and scraped his teeth across the base of her thumb. "Got a bucket of cold water handy?"

Her eyes narrowed. "If you're not interested in fucking, you can just say no. You don't have to threaten to dump cold water on me—"

He kissed her, but he was smiling too much to make it more than a quick peck. "Sweetness, the cold water ain't for you. Or for me. It's to dump on the fire."

"Oh. Uh, I think there's a cooler of ice under the picnic bench." She scrambled off his lap.

"I'll get it." He pushed out of the chair. "Keep that blanket away from the fire. When you go up in flames, I want it to be from my touch."

Her eyes took on a sensual, slumberous haze but she didn't say a single word.

Callie remained quiet and watchful as he doused the fire.

There wasn't sexy chatter between as she led him to her camper.

And when they were inside her cozy bedroom space, they were too busy mauling each other to talk.

The kisses were hard and wet and impatient.

Slow it down, buddy.

He ignored that warning and stripped to his boxers. Then he tugged Callie between his legs as he sat on the edge of her bed and watched as she peeled off her shirt. He couldn't get his mouth on her tits fast enough and she accidentally elbowed him in the face when she reached around to unhook her bra.

"Sorry. I'm just…"

"Me too," she whispered.

Justin groaned and bent to take her nipple in his mouth, twining his tongue around the tip, stopping to suck hard, and then starting all over again on the other side. Had he ever truly appreciated being with a young woman with firm, perky, luscious breasts? Even when he'd been a clueless kid in his twenties?

That's what you're thinking about? Why don't you take your creepy old man thoughts and tell her you're happy her boobs haven't started to sag yet like the older chicks you've fucked?

He shook his head to clear it and ended up motorboating her.

Not sexy or cool at all, old man.

What the hell was up with the running commentary from his subconscious?

She squeezed his shoulders for balance as he pushed her pants down the curve of her ass and past her knees. Stepping out of her jeans, she paused in front of him, acting a little shy.

"Tell me what you want," he said gruffly.

If you'd taken the time to get to know her before fucking her, you wouldn't even have to ask her.

"You have a condom?" she asked in a soft voice.

"Yep."

"Put it on."

Is she impatient because she wants to get this over with?

Shut up, stupid play by play.

"Spread your legs first," he urged. As soon as she complied, he brought her down to his thigh. "Rub yourself off. I wanna watch."

Callie started kissing up his neck, stopping at his ear. "I don't want to get myself off. I want you to get me off. I don't want to wait anymore."

"Stretch out on the bed."

When he found the condom in his jeans pocket, he dropped it twice before he got ahold of the package enough to rip it open and put it on.

She parted her legs and he scooted up on his knees, trailing his fingers up the silken expanse of her outer thigh.

He levered himself over her, grateful for the dark.

From that first deep thrust, Justin knew he was a goner.

A goner.

Totally gone for this girl.

If he kept going...he'd never want to leave the tight, wet heat of her body.

That's what she wants. She'll get her hooks in you and never let go.

The warning *too soon, too young* got louder and louder, drowning out everything else.

A burning sensation squeezed his lungs, expanding until he feared it'd tear him apart.

I can't breathe. Why the fuck can't I breathe?

Then he made the mistake of looking into Callie's eyes.

Something more than lust shone back at him.

Hope.

He blinked, trying to erase the expression he'd seen on her face, praying he'd misread it.

But at second glance, it hadn't changed.

It'd intensified.

Not that. Give me any look but that one. I'm not the man you think I am.

"Justin," she said softly. "Don't."

"I can't do this."

"Wait—"

But he didn't. He pulled out of her abruptly and scrambled off the bed.

Immediately the heat and urgency that had driven him to this point morphed into a cold sweat and he started to shake.

He found his clothes and dressed quickly, silently begging her to let him escape without discussing what a spectacular fuck-up this was.

It doesn't have to be. You can fix it.

No. Don't second-guess yourself. Just go.

When he heard her inhale, he braced himself.

"You're leaving?"

Justin gave her a curt nod and reached for his hat.

"Fucking me was that much of a disappointment?" she demanded.

"One thrust isn't fucking, Callie."

"What we were doing before that one *non*-fucking thrust...doesn't count?"

Justin lifted his chin. "All of it counts—"

"Don't say it," she warned.

"—as one big mistake," he finished.

"You don't mean that."

He didn't know what the fuck he meant. Or what he wanted...except to get out so he could breathe. So he could think. Maybe then he could silence the voices warring inside his head.

"I'm sorry."

She didn't say one word in return.

Yell at me, call me names, because you know how to get to me.

Talk about sending himself mixed messages. He couldn't stay but he didn't want to go.

Fear won out over hope. It always did for him.

His boots barely touched the floor as he ran out.

Chapter Seven

It'd been five weeks since Justin had pulled the one-pump chump dump.

Five long, confusing weeks.

Sometimes Callie had to remind herself they'd only been together three days before the implosion, explosion, whatever it was called that'd caused the shift between them.

Why had those three days seemed like three weeks? She'd never clicked with a man like that before. It'd sliced her down to the bone when he'd just left her like that, after she'd opened herself up to him emotionally and physically.

She had no one to talk to about it—her sisters were in their own little worlds; her mom would worry that she'd gotten mixed up with a "broke-down cowboy," so Callie had turned to the internet for advice. Those experts who offered assurances that deep cuts healed faster were full of shit. That single cut had expanded like a crack in a windshield, until it was big enough to shatter her outer shell.

So here she was for the first time in her life, walking around with her heart unprotected, with her defenses down completely, and that fucker Justin Donohue was clueless about it.

Talk about fucked-up. Callie was pretty sure that you were supposed to hate a guy after he did something like that, not understand why he did it, and hope the dumbass came to his senses.

The next morning, she allowed herself one hour to mope and cry. Then she did what she always had: picked herself up and went to work. Her life would go on whether or not he chose to be a part of it for the next couple of months.

Running into him the first time...Callie acted no differently toward him. She neither went out of her way to talk to him or avoid him. With the rodeo school in session that first week, they barely saw each other at the compound.

But Justin showed up every night she worked at The Sly Fox.

He never approached her. Never tipped her. Never tossed money on the bar after she danced. In fact, he went out of his way to lurk in a dark corner with his cowboy hat angled to hide his face.

She had to secretly laugh at that. Did he really think she wouldn't notice him? Everyone took notice of a man who typified brooding cowboy loner.

Week two of their breakup or breakdown, or whatever it was...Callie got assigned to work the arena where the bull riding instruction took place. She finally got to see two-time PBR world champion Justin Donohue on the back of a bull.

His first ride was shit. But his second ride...Jesus, Joseph, and Mary. The man defined grace and raw power. She stood there like a total newb, her mouth open, her tongue hanging out, goosebumps covering her body.

He finished the ride with a text-book dismount—landing on his booted feet in the dirt with his Stetson still on his head.

Their eyes met across the fence. The cocky fucker was perfectly aware of her swooning reaction. After bestowing a wicked grin that made her damn nipples hard, he tipped his hat at her, as if he'd dedicated the ride to her.

That's when things got really weird.

Starting the next day, Justin tracked her down and ate lunch in the cafeteria with her. Every day. Didn't matter who she was with—Lana, Bill, or Dickie—he joined in, acting his friendly charming self. Asking her questions, offering up stories about his students, or what'd happened with Deke during a stock check. He treated her like a friend, a buddy, not a guy who'd briefly put his dick in her, found it not to his liking, and bailed.

During one of their lunches, he'd overheard her talking to London Grant about her love of lemon-flavored candies and baked goods. From that day forward, she'd find a lemon-flavored goodie in her locker in the employee breakroom. Every day.

Someone placed two new pots of flowers around her fifth-wheel.

Someone brought over a stack of firewood for the bonfires that were becoming a Sunday night tradition among the Grade A employees.

Someone fixed the broken window on her camper.

The someone part wasn't a mystery. The mystery was *why* Justin did all that.

Callie didn't know what to make of it. If it were anyone else, she'd ask what the hell was going on. But part of her feared if she asked him, he'd stop.

Instead, he stepped up his efforts to…deepen their friendship. That was the most logical explanation because the man hadn't made a move on her at all.

On Friday movie afternoons, he begged her to help him chaperone the students. They shared popcorn and snarky comments about the lame "wholesome" type of western movies.

When he discovered she headed for the gym on the nights she couldn't sleep, he showed up to run alongside her on the treadmill. She suspected he synched his wireless headset to her MP3 just so he could complain about her taste in music. He'd never heard of One Direction, Ed Sheeran, Sia, or Imagine Dragons. Callie called him old and he'd just laughed.

The next time they worked out together, he'd forced her to listen to his music. She never would have guessed that a forty-year-old white cowboy from South Dakota loved Eminem, NIN, Metallica, Snoop, and TLC. He found some amusement when she serenaded him with "No Scrubs."

In the meantime, Lana and Deke had started dating and she had to listen to her friend blather on about her new boyfriend. Callie didn't believe it'd last, but she wasn't the type to burst Lana's happy bubble just because she was confused about her own situation with Justin. In fact, she oughta get nominated for the Friend Hall of Fame for lending Deke and Lana her camper the night Lana decided to let Deke pop her cherry.

But that was a double-edged sword: it seemed she and Justin were always covering for the lovebirds. Callie got roped into doing the first cattle check at least twice a week so Deke and Lana could be together. But she hadn't minded. She loved being outdoors. And watching Justin on horseback was worth losing sleep over; the man was a sight to behold in chaps and spurs. If he'd draped a coil of rope over the saddle horn, she might've had a spontaneous orgasm.

So they'd become close…as close as two people could be who were rarely alone together since the rodeo school was a chaotic place 24/7.

Callie figured that's why Justin still came to the bar a couple of times a week—he needed adult entertainment that required no interaction on his part. He didn't stay long and he was always gone when she clocked out.

Then earlier this week, she was surprised to see him in the parking lot when her shift ended at one a.m.

She enjoyed the view for a moment, his tight, jeans-clad cowboy ass sticking out as he bent at the waist under the hood. "Justin?"

He banged his head he stood up so fast. "Ow. Fuck."

"Sorry. What's going on?"

"I have no fucking idea." He ran a grease-covered hand through his hair in a move she recognized as pure frustration. "It won't start. It ain't the battery, or the spark plugs or the timing chain."

"Has it been acting up?"

"Yeah. I was gonna get it to the garage as soon as I…" He glanced at her with embarrassment.

His pride wouldn't let him admit he didn't have the cash to get it fixed. "Nothing you can do about it tonight. Lucky for you I can give you a ride back to the ranch." She pointed at the mysterious parts strewn across a tarp on the ground. "Need help picking that up?"

"I have half a mind to use the tarp to set the whole thing on fire. Piece of shit."

"It's late, you're tired. It'll look different in the morning."

"You're probably right." Justin rolled up the tarp and tossed it into the back of his truck.

She pulled around to pick him up.

"Thanks for the ride."

"You're welcome. Have you been out there messing around with it since you left the bar two hours ago?"

"Yeah. I'm not mechanically inclined. I can see basic problems, but this one…?" He shook his head. "Who knows what it'll take to fix it."

Or how much money. Money she suspected he didn't have. "If it's a major issue, I'm sure Chuck and Berlin would advance you—"

Justin held up his hand. "Let's talk about something else. Please."

But the silence stretched between them.

She couldn't ask any of the questions she wanted to.

Why do you come into the bar and leave without talking to me? To remind yourself that I'm young and I have a job where other men leer at me? Does that cool down your attraction for me?

Why haven't we ever talked about the night you took off? Why are you so sweet and thoughtful to me now? Is it just to make me want what I can't have?

"Callie," he said sharply.

"What?"

"Watch the road."

"Sorry. I was lost in thought."

"I know where your mind went," he said softly. "Look, it's time I explain why I—"

"Stop right there." She realized she didn't have the heart or mindset to deal with this discussion now. "I'm exhausted and weaving all over the damn road, so I don't have enough functioning bran cells to concentrate on that type of discussion. Can we just listen to the radio?"

"Fine."

Classic country filled the cab, but she didn't pay attention. She felt Justin staring at her, and she ignored that too.

Callie pulled up to her camp spot and put her truck in park. She opened her duffel bag, fishing out a wad of bills—her tips from this week. Then she thrust the money at Justin. "Here. Don't argue with me. Take it and get your truck fixed. Pay me back when you can."

"Jesus, Callie. No. I don't need—"

"Yes, you do. Swallow your pride, cowboy hottie. This loan will be our little secret, okay?" She looked away from his intense gaze. "We've all been there. I've been broke more often than not. You'd do the same for me, wouldn't you?"

He cleared his throat. "Yeah, sweetness, I would."

"Then it's settled." She opened the driver's side door and jumped down. "And take my truck. You'll need it tomorrow during the day. I won't."

"You're sure?"

"Positive."

"I won't forget this, Callie. I owe you. Anytime you need something, all you gotta do is ask."

"I will. Now I gotta get some sleep. I'll see you tomorrow."

Except she hadn't seen him the next day. Or the day after that.

But he had left her freshly-washed truck parked in her usual spot, the tank full of gas.

And now, she'd test that *anytime you need something* statement right now.

Callie scrolled down her list of messages. She and Justin had texted each other once, right after she'd given him her number, he'd sent her a smiley-face emoji with the word *hey*. Hopefully he hadn't deleted her contact info.

ME: Hey, it's Callie. You have time to help me out?

His response was immediate.

JD: Yep. Whatcha need?

ME: A distraction. Are you working Stirling's surprise party tonight?

JD: I'm supposed to pick her up at the house in the ATV in 20. Why?

ME: I'm waiting with her. Except she brought a surprise guest, her boyfriend and the minute they're out of the bedroom, she'll insist on going to the barn early and Mrs. G will KILL me if I don't keep her outta there until everything is ready. We gotta stall until we get the all clear.

JD: So you want me to be late?

ME: NO, she'll hop in her car and drive herself. We need to get them away from here so they're stuck with us and can't escape.

JD: Tall order, sweetness. You got a plan?

ME: I'm gonna pick a fight with you first thing. And no matter what I say, play along. Give it right back to me.

JD: Baby girl, I'll give it to you real good :)

Her belly did that little flip, swirl thingy. Surely he hadn't meant it that way?

Or maybe he had.

She'd think about it later. She had a fight to stage.

* * * *

Justin pulled up in the ATV right on time. Looking like a million bucks. He probably smelled good too, as Callie could see he was clean shaven.

He hopped out and offered his hand to Stirling's boyfriend. "Hey. I'm Justin. I work at the Gradsky Ranch. You must be Stirling."

Callie about lost it. That was a perfect choice to start off this comedy of errors. She stomped down the stairs. "Are you kidding me right now? *That* is Stirling." She pointed at the blonde woman sporting dreads almost to her waist. "She is Chuck and Berlin's *daughter*."

Silence.

Justin faced Stirling, his handsome face tomato red. "I am sorry, Miss Gradsky. No offense. I've only worked here a few weeks. I'm still figuring things out."

"No worries. This is my partner, Liam Argent."

"Pleasure to meet you, sir."

"You as well, Justin."

"We probably better get goin'."

But Liam forgot something in the house—thank goodness that'd eat up some time—and Stirling walked across the porch, taking in the view while she waited for her boyfriend. Since she wasn't paying attention to them…showtime.

"God. Do you have to be so embarrassing?" Callie hissed at Justin, loud enough for Stirling to hear. "You thought *Stirling* was a guy? That is not a guy's name."

"What about Sterling Sharpe, who played for the Packers? Or Sterling Archer?"

Callie turned her laugh into a huff of annoyance then she gave Justin the signal to keep it going.

"Wow. So you *don't* know everything. Next time you spout off, little girl, remind yourself you could learn a thing or two from your elders."

Little girl? That stung.

When Justin discreetly cupped his balls and smirked, telling her that he remembered her threat, she relaxed. He was playing a part, same as she was.

Liam exited the house sooner than Callie expected.

He said, "Sorry. I'm ready."

Justin gestured for their guests to sit in the back. He took his sweet time rechecking the mirrors and the gauges on the dashboard.

Right after they started tooling down the paved path, Callie turned around and addressed Liam. "So what kind of doctor are you? Because I have this rash—"

"I'm not a medical doctor. I have a doctorate in microbiology."

Callie gave him a comical, confused look. "To be honest, I'm not even sure what that means. Sounds like a class I probably would've skipped."

"Or failed," Justin added with a snicker.

She pushed his shoulder. "Shut it and drive. I wasn't talking to you."

"I could be so fuckin' lucky," he shot back.

Their passengers exchanged a WTF? look. But Stirling was too polite to get involved.

"What sort of work do you do for my parents?" Stirling asked.

"Whatever they want me to do." She smiled and confided, "This week I've mostly been cleaning. Last week I filled in as a ranch hand with grumpy over there." She pointed with her head to Justin and paused long enough that he could take his eyes off the road and scowl at her. "Next week I might be takin' care of the animals."

A glazed look came over Stirling's face.

Just as Callie was about to bore them with more mundane details of her life, the ATV hit a bump.

Callie went airborne and bit back the urge to yell at Justin that forcing an injury wasn't part of the stalling plan. She scrambled for a hold on the roll bar as Justin hit the brakes and snagged the back of her jacket—both of which kept her from bouncing out on her head.

"Would you please park your ass in the seat?" Justin snapped. "You about gave me a goddamned heart attack."

Peering into his eyes, she realized he wasn't faking his anger. She mouthed "I'm okay" and he exhaled.

Not that their passengers noticed.

Justin elbowed her.

She rolled her eyes. "I'm fine. Keep movin', Daddy-o. We're on Berlin time and if we're late, I'm rolling on you."

Stirling covered a laugh with a cough.

Callie half turned in the seat and looked from Liam to Stirling. Now they both looked a little...glazed. Wait, were they high?

"Do I have lipstick on my teeth or something?" Stirling said with total paranoia.

Jesus. They *were* both high. Well, they did work in a dispensary. And them being a little out of it would make this situation seem bizarre anyway, so no need to hold back. "No. And this will sound weird, but your mom has been telling me about all the awesome things you've done and how you were driven to succeed even when you were a kid." She paused. "That sounds just like my little sister Chelsea. Not the dreads or the kickin' clothes, but she has that same drive."

"Really?"

"Yeah. Chels is a soccer player, not a business whiz like you. She's dying to play pro soccer now, but our mom is like...you are going to college first."

"You shoulda listened to your mom too," Justin said.

"There wasn't money for me to go college. Besides, nothin' wrong with bein' a bartender."

"You're tendin' bar tonight too?" Justin demanded. "On your night off from bartending?"

"Yep. See if you can keep up, old man."

Justin grunted.

Callie's cell phone buzzed.

Shit. She read the message KEEP STALLING from Mrs. G and showed it to Justin, in the guise of elbowing him as she said, "Change of plans. Take the shortcut."

"What shortcut?"

"That one." Callie pointed the opposite direction.

"That is *not* a shortcut."

"Yes, it is! Turn now or we'll miss it."

Justin hit the brakes. He patted the steering wheel. "See this? This means *I* decide which way we're going, shortstuff, not you. And we ain't takin' what you call the shortcut."

Shortstuff? That was a new nickname. "You are so stubborn!"

"Like that's news," Justin scoffed.

They started moving again...at a crawl.

"You are doing this on purpose," she said with false anger, ignoring the panicked whispers of their passengers.

"Safety first, little girl."

"Omigod, I am not a little girl! You make me want to scream!"

Justin pointedly ignored her, a smug look on that handsome mug.

Despite this being a ruse, it brought to mind all of Callie's frustrations with this man.

He just kept putzing along—in the ATV and he'd been doing the same damn thing with their relationship or whatever it was the past five weeks.

She truly wanted to scream at him to wake the fuck up and look at her. See her.

And this was her chance.

Callie leaned over and screamed in Justin's ear.

It didn't faze him at all.

He just muttered, "I can't fucking believe you did that."

Since their passengers were whispering back and forth, Callie angled closer so only Justin could hear her. "I've wanted to do that for five goddamned weeks."

He shot her a look. "Yeah? Join the club."

"I can't do this with you right now. We have other things to deal with."

"But we will be doin' something about this later, Callie. Guaranteed. This time I ain't letting it go."

"Whatever." She spun around and said, "So how long have you two been together?"

Liam said, "And she's *baaaaack*," under his breath...or what a high person considered a quiet tone, but both Justin and Callie heard him.

Justin snickered.

"Gosh, what's it been...seven days?" Stirling cooed.

"Eight fantastic days," Liam corrected with a growl.

And these two being so damn cutesy together...after not being together for very long...annoyed her. "Does London know you've got a boyfriend? Because I thought she planned to fix you up with someone."

"Callie, shut up," Justin snarled. "You don't say shit like that to people. Your mama raised you better than that."

"What? I'm just making conversation."

The recreation center came into view as they rounded the corner.

"Here's where we exit this crazy train," Stirling said. "Let us out here. We'll walk."

"No can do. Our orders are front door delivery," Justin said.

"Since when do you follow orders?" Callie demanded. "You do things on your own time frame—"

Stirling released an ear-piercing whistle.

Startled, Justin slammed on the brakes.

"Here's a piece of advice." Sterling bailed out and paused by the curb. "Working with family is the hardest thing you'll do. I work with my brother every day. Sometimes I want to scream at him. But I don't *lit-er-al-ly* scream at him. Our disagreements happen behind closed doors. Never in front of employees or customers. I can see that your dad embarrasses you, Calliope, and it probably sucks working together so closely because he treats you like a child—"

"Whoa, whoa, whoa there. Justin is not my *dad*."

Justin had lost his sense of humor about the entire thing. He pointed at Callie. "I told you that's what people would think. I *told* you. That's why—"

"You're a chickenshit, Justin Donohue. And like I told you, I don't care what people think. I'm getting out now too."

He snapped, "Like hell you are," and hit the gas.

Chapter Eight

"Justin, what are you doing? Stop this damn thing right now!"

"Nope."

Callie tightened her grip on the roll bar because he was driving like a freakin' maniac. "I'll scream again."

"Do it if it makes you feel better."

"The only thing that'll make me feel better is getting back to the barn and doing my goddamned job! This party is for the Gradskys' daughter. If they ever have cause to fire me it'll be if I don't show up to work at a family party."

Justin pulled out his phone.

"Put both of your hands back on the wheel right now!"

He didn't—but he did slow down.

"Deke," he barked into the phone. "Get to the barn and tell anyone who asks that you're filling in as a bartender. Yes, now. Callie's not feeling well and we've covered for you so it's time for you to repay the favor." His jaw tightened. "I don't give a damn if Lana comes too, but get your ass down there now. That is not a request, that's an order from your boss." He hung up.

Do not get all swoony about how hot he is when he's acting bossy.

She wasn't surprised when he pulled up to her camper. There weren't many places they could be alone.

Justin's eyes challenged her. "You walkin' in on your own? Because I swear to God, Callie, if you try and run, I'll put you over my knee and spank you after I catch you."

"It'd almost be worth it to see how fast you can run, old timer," she retorted.

He exhaled. "I'm tryin' hard to keep my cool, sweetness. Really fucking hard. So can we please just go inside?"

"Fine." She dug her key out of her front pocket and opened the door.

When she stood aside to let him go in first, he grinned. "Nice try, baby girl, but I'll be locking the door after we're *both* inside."

"Whatever."

And Justin did lock the door behind him. He seemed at a loss as he faced her. Taking in his surroundings killed another thirty seconds. "This is a really great place, Callie. Did you remodel it yourself?"

"Yes. And you were in here before."

"Didn't see much, if you'll recall, since it was dark and we pretty much went straight to your bed."

"Yeah. I guess you wouldn't have taken time to look around before you ran out that night."

There. Now the elephant was front and center in the room.

"I'm sorry. It was a dick move."

"Wrong. It was a *non*-dicking move."

Justin moved forward. Spun around. Moved back. "I can't pace in here either."

"Either?"

"It's fourteen steps in my room at the bunkhouse before I have to turn around and start over. Trust me I've counted. I've done a lot of pacing in the past few weeks." He looked at her. "Can we start now? Been killin' me to just let it lie."

"Killing you? We've been together every day for the past five weeks. Every day! You had plenty of time to start this conversation with me. Plenty."

"I wanted it to be private."

"Because God forbid that someone might overhear us." She tried to sound mad…but it was just so damn humiliating that he didn't want anyone to know they'd been together even one time.

"Callie—"

His near-patronizing tone had her bristling. "Tell me why, after we got naked together—which was inevitable from the moment we met—that you couldn't even wait until you got off to run out like your ass was on fire?" She paused, trying to keep her voice from breaking. "Did I say something wrong? Did I do something you didn't like? Even if I smelled bad or something, I need to know why that happened." She fought another wave of mortification, hating that she sounded so damn vulnerable.

"You didn't smell bad, for fuck's sake." He inhaled a deep breath and let it out. "It smells like you in here. Sweet and flowery and womanly. I love that."

"Justin. That's not helping."

"This ain't gonna be easy to admit, all right?" He unclenched his jaw. "I ran out because it hit me that I'd known you for three fucking days. I liked you, I lusted after you, I worked with you, I was pissed off that I'm too old for you...everything that was right and wrong between us became a loud noise in my head. A warning I couldn't ignore. And yeah, it sucked that it didn't start screaming at me until the worst possible moment."

"When you were inside me," she said bluntly.

He winced. "Like I said, worst possible moment. I wish I could say I had an attack of conscience or some altruistic shit and that's why I stopped, but I've since figured out it was a panic attack." His cheeks burned bright red. "Christ. I'm a forty-year-old man, not a kid. I've never had a panic attack in my life, not on the back of a bull, not when they interviewed me on TV. So the fact I experienced one when I was balls deep in a woman I wanted more than my next fucking breath...I had do what my head told me and not listen to my what my dick wanted."

What could she even say to that? Him panicking made no sense to her, and the fact it made no sense to him either...Callie had to believe he wasn't feeding her full of shit.

"Afterward, when I was still walkin' around in a damn daze because I felt guilty for leaving you the way I had, I knew I couldn't be with you until I straightened some things out. My issues. Not yours. None of this is your fault, Callie. I've had enough fuck and forget encounters to last me a lifetime." When he finally looked at her, she saw his conflicting emotions had turned his eyes a stormy blue. "I didn't want it to be that way with you."

"What makes you think it would have been?" She swallowed the hard lump in her throat. "I told you I wasn't looking for anything more than just fun naked times with you. I thought that's what we both wanted."

He nodded. "I did. I mean...I do. But that's the worst thing I could've done, continuing to...be intimate with you as that greedy, selfish guy."

And he still didn't get it. "Wrong. Leaving how you did was the worst thing you could've done to me." Goddammit why did her voice warble now when she needed to show him she could roll with the punches—even when his running out had felt like a punch in the gut. His claims that his actions were his issues didn't change the fact that his issues brought her own insecurities to the surface.

Maybe it was a good thing he hadn't stuck around to see them.

Needing a moment to regroup, Callie walked to the tiny kitchen and peered out the window. Dusk had fallen, blanketing the world in shades of pinkish orange. This was her favorite time of day—Justin's too. She hadn't known that five weeks ago. She hadn't known anything about him except that overwhelming feeling of lust whenever they were together. So part of her did understand his abrupt and humiliating change of mind because they'd basically been strangers. Now they weren't.

"Callie?"

"Sorry, just thinking." She pulled out two bottles of water from the fridge, handed one to him and settled on the couch. "Park it. You're making me nervous."

He sat. "Talk to me."

She sighed. "As weird as the panic attack thing is, I'm happy that you didn't pull out the 'I'm a special little snowflake' excuse."

"I don't even know what the hell that is."

"Come on, you know the lame-ass line that a guy uses, 'you're too hot, too sweet, too perfect, too special' when he's not into me. He makes it seem like he was doing me a *favor* by not fucking me." She took a sip of water. "It blows."

Justin scowled. "Sounds like all men are as goddamned dumb as I am when it comes to you."

Oh. That was sort of...sweet.

"If I could charm my way out of this confusing mess with you, I would. That's my default reaction." His gaze bored into her. "But none of my actions around you are normal. I've had to face some hard truths about my age bein' a factor."

"Meaning what?"

"Meaning I judged *you* based on *my* life experiences when I was twenty-two. Just because I didn't have my shit together and partied my ass off, doesn't mean you're the same. A twenty-two-year-old woman I dated when I was that same age turned out to be slightly psycho, especially after I broke things off with her. All this stuff was churning below the surface with me, stuff I'd forgotten about, but I needed to remember my past to deal with my present."

His obsession with her age made more sense. "What conclusion did you come to?"

"I like you too much to stay away from you."

Callie snorted. "That's why you came into the bar and didn't say a word to me? Because you *liked* me too much?"

Justin reached out, snagging a section of her hair. "I came to the bar because I like to watch you dance."

"Looking and not touching cleared up your confusion?"

"Yeah, it did. I realized as much as I wanted your hot little body nine ways 'til Sunday, I wanted to get to know you first. Not in a dating type situation, because I totally would've fucked that up, but getting to know you as a coworker and a friend."

"I'm not being flip when I say I never wanted to be your friend...but I liked it when you forced the issue."

His eyebrow rose. "Forced the issue?"

"Lunch together every day ringing a bell?"

He fiddled with the piece of hair he'd grabbed. "Then you'll really be pissed off that I forced the issue with Chuck and Berlin, asking them to assign you to arena one with me."

"You asked them that?"

"They agreed. You're better with stock than anyone else. I knew that Breck would snap you up to work with him, so I made sure I got to you first."

Oh you got to me all right.

"During the mundane stuff, you talked to me. I was damn near giddy about that. Because it proved me right. That I liked you, not just because I lusted after you and was tryin' to justify it."

"Good for you, Justin. You've had several moments of personal growth in the past five weeks."

He narrowed his eyes at her sarcasm.

"While you were judging me, I was just as busy judging myself. You thought I was easy because I went to bed with you three days after we met. You came into the bar and watched me work to convince yourself I acted too young to get involved with, or to convince yourself that I was old enough to know what I was doing and it'd be all right to fuck me as long as no one knew we were fucking."

"You done?" he said coolly when she took a breath.

"I don't know. If I think about it, it makes me sad."

That threw him. "Sad? Not mad?"

"I'm sad for you because you're so…worried about what other people think that you're missing out on a good thing." She locked her gaze to his. "Me. I am a good person. I work hard, I try and have a little fun when I can. I have goals and I've always been able to take care of myself. I'm not an old soul or any of that bullshit, but I haven't had the life of a typical twenty-two-year-old. But all you see is the number when you look at me."

"That might've been true five weeks ago, but it ain't true now. As I've explained." He stood and gently hauled her to her feet. "What do you see when you look at me, Callie?"

"Sex on legs," she blurted out. "You think you're the only one with lustful thoughts?"

Liquid heat replaced the wariness in his eyes. "Are we done talkin' about this?"

"I am as long as we're both finally on the same page."

"Which page is that, sweetness?"

"Lots of exclusive nekkid time while we're both here. No promises, no regrets."

Justin granted her that dirty-wicked grin and fuck-me eyes and her stomach flipped. "Sign. Me. Up." He captured her mouth and kissed her until her knees gave out.

Then he hooked his arms under her legs and carried into her bedroom.

After settling her on the edge of the bed, he pressed his back against the wall. "Undress yourself for me. Show me what I'm dyin' to take."

"Maybe I want you to undress me."

"I don't wanna rip your clothes. Because I'm so far gone for you that I'm hanging by a thread as it is."

Oh, there was the sexual boost she needed. No surprise it'd come from him.

Callie watched his molten eyes as he watched her.

First she shook out her hair.

That earned her a muscle tic in his jaw.

She unbuttoned her blouse, not exactly slowly but making sure he anticipated the deftness in her fingers as she slipped the button free from the hole, stroked the placket, and moved to the next. Soon as the shirt hung open, she peeled it down her arms and tossed it in his face.

Justin caught it and held it up, breathing deeply and closing his eyes.

Damn, that was sexy. She couldn't wait to toss her panties at him.

She perched on the edge of her bed and yanked off her boots. Taking two steps to the modified closet, she bent at the waist and dropped them on the floor, giving Justin a good look at her ass. Then she gave him an even better look at her ass as she shimmied her jeans off.

That earned her a growl.

When Callie faced him again, just in her bra and panties, she struck a pin-up girl pose. "Like what you see, bull rider?"

"Fuck yeah."

"You want me to take these last two pieces of clothing off? Or would you like to do the honors?"

"Take off the panties first," he gritted out.

"Do you want to know if I'm wet?" she said huskily. "If baring my body for you turns me on?"

"Does it?"

"The look in your eyes does it for me. I love seeing that you wanna do dirty things to me. Here's a secret. I want you to do dirty things to me too."

One blond brow winged up. "You sure about that?"

"Positive. See, I've only been with guys my age, maybe a few years older. They have no imagination. I want a man—I want you—to use your years of sexual experience to show me what I've been missing. I'd like to be tied up. Or tied down. I'd like to feel the sting of your palm on my ass. I want you to spread me out on the table and go down on me until your face is so wet from my juices that it's running down your neck. I want to blow you in a restaurant bathroom just because I can't wait another second to make your eyes roll back in your head. I want you to fuck me in the shower. Against the wall. On my knees in the pasture. On my back in your tiny dorm room with your hand over my mouth so no one knows how loud you make me scream when you fuck me. All the dirty things we do to each other ain't nobody's business but ours."

Justin muttered something that came out a primitive growl.

The hair on the back of Callie's neck stood up as desire pulsed from him. She continued to taunt him, pushing her panties to her knees, turning around, placing her palms flat on the bed and peering at him over her shoulder. "You want me like this. Hobbled a little. Gives you more control and makes everything...tighter. But I wonder...would you have those big, callused hands of yours in my hair? Or would you need to have them gripping my hips because you're fucking me so hard you need something to hold on to?"

He swallowed hard. Twice.

Oh, goody, this was fun.

She swayed her hips as if she was dancing, put her arms above her head, and turned around.

His eyes watched every sway of her tits.

"Then there are these." She cupped her breasts. "I know you're a tit man. I wonder if I'll have to remind you once you've got your hands and mouth on them, that there are other parts of me worthy of such devotion."

"Don't you worry, I ain't forgetting that anytime soon."

She unhooked her bra and tossed it behind her. She lifted her breasts up and smashed them together.

He sucked in a breath.

"I know how badly you want to slide your cock in here. I'll love every thrust and grind and stroke. I'll even love it when you blow your load all over me."

"I'm done, Callie. I can't take any more."

Perching on the edge of the bed, she spread her legs wide, placing her palms on her knees and arching her back. "Your turn, cowboy hottie. Strip for me."

Justin's greedy gaze continued to scan her body as he absentmindedly removed his clothes. First he undid the snaps on the cuffs of his shirt, then he tugged the shirttail out from his jeans and popped all eight buttons up the front of his shirt at one time. He shrugged it off in that sexy way that men did and draped it over the chair. One yank of his T-shirt and he was bare-chested.

"Lookit you, cowboy. All muscles and chest hair and more muscles."

His cocky grin doubled her need to get her grabby hands all over him.

Off went his boots.

And socks.

He undid his belt—a championship belt buckle this time, she noticed—but didn't unthread the leather from the loops of his jeans. Watching her eyes admiring his body, he lowered the zipper and ditched the jeans and his underwear in a single movement.

Callie sighed. "Cowboy hottie Justin Donohue in my bedroom, nekkid as the day he was born…except for his hat. I might've died and gone to heaven."

"You'll feel that way when I've got my mouth on your pussy." He stroked his cock as he took two steps forward.

Her gaze dropped to it. Big enough to feel good but not a monster cock that'd be painful to take. "Your dick is perfect."

"It's in perfect working order tonight."

"I can tell." She gazed up at him. "You are the hottest man I've ever seen."

"Callie."

The way he said her name sent shivers down her spine. "Do you have condoms?"

"One."

"Shoot. That's one more than I have."

He took off his hat. "Weren't expecting this?"

She shook her head.

"I've got a box in my room." He dropped to his knees. "I'll go get them later."

"Okay."

He smoothed his hands up the outside of her thighs. "Need me to take over now, sweetness?"

"Yes, please."

Justin pressed his lips to the inside of her knee. After the first kiss he planted another. And another. And another. Until the next place his mouth would land was where she most wanted it.

His hand nearly spanned her hips when he placed his palm over her belly button and pushed until she was sprawled on her back.

Callie's legs, abdomen, and chest vibrated from excitement.

He stroked her stomach with the backs of his knuckles and said, "Settle down, baby girl, I'm just getting started."

And he dove in—tongue, fingers and teeth.

The first orgasm happened so fast she was embarrassed.

She tried to sit up, he pushed her back down and went at her again. This time with more finesse. Those full lips of his were just soft enough and firm enough to rub along the outer rim while his tongue flicked the heart of her. She wanted his mouth on her clit and he was taking his sweet time about it. He'd treat her to a few soft sucks of her pussy lips, a few deep thrusts with his fingers, followed by that wet tongue licking and fucking its way inside her.

Her legs were back to shaking and she was openly begging him.

That's when he focused all of his attention on her clit. Sucking rhythmically and relentlessly, holding her down with both hands as she thrashed beneath him, pushing her to that line between pleasure and pain that she'd heard about but never experienced. He kept at her and kept at her until she broke apart. There was no rise, no ebb and flow. There was a KABOOM that left a deep throbbing in her core, a ringing in her ears and a tickle in her tailbone.

No wait. That was Justin tickling her tailbone.

She scrambled to her elbows. "That was…"

"I know, sweetness."

"How?"

"You're verbal when you come that hard." He smiled and kissed the inside of her still quivering thigh. "And loud. It's hot as fuck but it might scare the neighbors."

Callie groaned.

Justin rolled to his feet and took his cock in his hand. "I gotta rub one out or I won't last."

"You want me to—"

"No, I want you to watch." He started to stroke. Hard and fast and a bit violently. "That pussy of yours. So hot and sweet. Made me so fuckin' hard I have to do this." *Stroke, stroke, stroke.* "Get used to me bein' obsessed with that pussy." *Slap, slap, slap,* so loud she wondered if he was hurting himself. "I love eating it. I'm gonna love fucking it. And I'll be doin' both of them every chance I get."

"Justin—"

"Pinch your nipples," he growled. "I want them red and hard when I come on them."

Callie almost had another orgasm when he unloaded on her. Hearing his guttural moan of satisfaction. Watching the come shoot out the end of his cock. Feeling the heat of his release on her skin before it cooled and slid down the slope of her breast. She'd never had a man do that before. Never wanted it. But seeing the adoration shining in Justin's eyes…she'd do anything he wanted to see that look over and over again.

He kept his cock in his hand, finishing with little punches of his hips into his fist.

"Callie."

She tore her gaze away from his still rigid dick.

"You liked that."

"I loved that."

Relief swam in his eyes. He used his free hand to wipe away the droplet of come dangling on the tip of her nipple. Then he rubbed that sticky thumb across her bottom lip.

Immediately her tongue darted out to taste it. To taste him.

Then Justin was on her, pinning her arms to the mattress, kneeing her thighs apart, finding her opening, and driving inside her so hard her back bowed off the bed.

He went still.

Oh hell no. Not again.

Using every bit of strength, she bucked up. And catching him off guard allowed her to roll and push him to his back.

Callie eyed his dick, now resting on his lower belly and still as hard as before. She squeezed his hips with her knees as she leaned over him and they were face-to-face. "Going somewhere, cowboy?"

Confusion crossed his face. "Jesus. What the hell just happened?"

"You acted like you were gonna bail again."

"No! I stopped because I thought maybe I'd hurt you." He pushed her hair over her shoulder. "Did I?"

"Nope. But it did remind me of two things. First, we skipped the condom. And dude, that can't happen. I'm not on the pill. I have no problem going on it now, but until we're protected, no glove, no love. Period."

"Shit. Sorry. What's the second thing?"

"I'm gonna be on top in case you get any stupid ideas about taking off again."

He smiled and kissed her. "No way, sweetness. I'm sticking."

"Good."

When Callie reached for the condom he'd tossed on the dresser, Justin sat up and took her breasts in his hand, lowering his head to lick her nipples. Nipples that he'd come on not five minutes ago.

She snickered.

He managed to take his eyes and mouth off her tits long enough to say, "What?"

"I can't believe I called you a prude."

"Yeah. I am kind of a pervert."

"Mmm. I can't wait until you teach me all the ways I can be one too." She rolled the condom on him, kissed him, and reached between them to guide him inside.

They both groaned when she began to move.

Panting against her throat, Justin said, "You fuck just like you dance."

She slapped his ass. "Less talking. More fucking."

He flipped her onto her back and drove her out of her mind until that moment of bliss when they spiraled and tumbled into pleasure together.

They were kissing and stroking and just basking in the afterglow, the joy of being together like this, knowing it'd only get better.

Callie sighed. "You know I have to show up and work at that party for a little while."

"I know. We need to get more condoms and return the golf cart anyway."

He lifted off of her and she grabbed his arm. "You are coming back here with me tonight though, right?"

"Sweetness, you'll never get rid of me now. Chances are high my shit will be moved in by tomorrow."

She touched his face. "I can't wait."

* * * *

Later that night, after they'd done their duties at the party, reloaded on condoms, and were lying in Callie's bed, Callie blissed out from the third time Justin had fucked her tonight—once on the floor, once against the wall, once from behind on the bed—she said, "I have to ask you something."

"Shoot."

"Why'd you pull away from me tonight when Stirling and Liam caught us getting cozy behind the bar?"

Justin angled his head to look at her. "I thought we were still messin' with them."

She shook her head.

"Why do you care what they think, Callie? You're the one who told me to say *fuck off* to people who question what's goin' on between us."

"Sometimes I really hate that you listen to me so well," she grumbled.

"No you don't." He paused and toyed with her mouth—drawing her into a kiss with such raw sensuality it left her dizzy. "Hey, what's up with them calling you Calliope? She get your name wrong and you didn't correct her?"

"Here's where I remind you they were both high. But the truth is I was so nervous about getting them to the party without blowing the surprise, anxious about seeing you and starting the fight, that I introduced myself with my given name, which I never do because I don't like it."

"Wait. Calliope is your real name?"

"Calliope Jane. Ugh. You can see why I'd rather go by Callie."

He kissed her nose. "I kind of like it."

"Justin. You're avoiding the question."

"You pulled away from me too, when they caught us." His kisses moved to her cheek. Then her jaw. Then the tip of her chin. "We're together now. You know it. I know it. No one else matters. You're the one who told me that. And baby girl, I'm takin' that advice to heart."

"But—"

"Calliope," he said huskily, "no more talking."

* * * *

At the next staff meeting, the groups were sitting in their respective rows.

Callie wasn't looking for Justin. He'd gotten up at the crack of nothing and half the time he skipped the staff meetings.

But then, there he was, striding across the arena, boots kicking up dirt.

He said, "Sorry I'm late" to Chuck and Berlin as he passed by them.

He climbed over the fence and hoofed it up the arena steps.

Past the instructors' row.

Past the ranch hands' row.

He stopped at the maintenance crew's row. He said, "Hey," and caged Callie into her seat, bending down to press his lips to hers in a lingering kiss. Then he smiled at Lana. "Mind movin' over?"

No one else matters my ass.

But she knew he'd done it for her, letting everyone know they were together.

That's when the last piece clicked into place and Callie knew without a doubt that she was falling for him.

Chapter Nine

Justin paced in Callie's camper, wondering if this phone call was really necessary.

Maybe he should just spring it on his brother the next time Jack was in Denver. Show up with Callie, like it was no big deal that he'd fallen in love.

But it was a big deal. A *huge* deal.

The past two months had been amazing. Getting to know Callie on a platonic level and then sharing the type of intimacy with her that he never thought he'd find. Not just the sex, although that blew his freakin' mind every damn time, but just being with his sweet, sassy, sexy cowgirl. Doing normal couple things. Sharing meals. Sitting by the bonfire, drinking beer and swapping life stories with their coworkers. Curling up together watching TV on her rare nights off. Talking about everything, laughing about nothing, making love until they collapsed in a sweaty, sated pile and fell asleep in each other's arms. Justin was so gone for her that he even looked forward to doing laundry, grocery shopping and cleaning the camper with her.

Crazy to think he'd almost passed this up out of concern that he and Callie wouldn't have anything in common except their mutual lust. But she hadn't lied about being able to read him. She knew when he needed space and she could pull him out of his brooding thoughts like no one else had ever bothered to try.

The one wrinkle in their relationship was Callie refused to talk about their future, probably because she believed they didn't have one. Early on she'd promised him that she wasn't expecting long term—that she fully believed that he'd just move on to the next job in the next town. Any time he'd tried to broach the subject with her, she'd distracted him with her mouth or her smokin' hot body. And he'd let himself be distracted because his woman was very inventive in her dirty distraction techniques. But time was running out to tell her how he felt about her and ask for the chance to build a future with her. He still hadn't shared the fact that he had a hefty bank account, not out of fear she'd start to use him for his money, but fear that she'd see the gap in their financial statuses as a bigger issue than the gap in their ages and use it as an excuse to leave him.

Christ. He didn't know what he'd do if she left him.

Then you'd better figure out a way to make her want to stay with you.

Which led him back to his phone call because he needed advice.

Justin swiped over to his messages and scrolled down. Whoa. It'd been a while since he'd talked to his brother.

ME: Hey, big bro, you got time to talk?

Before the . . . appeared, his phone buzzed in his hand.

Caller ID: Jack.

He pressed accept call and answered, "That was fast."

"I assumed this was a ransom call from your kidnappers or you were finally ready to admit you've been in jail and that's why I haven't heard from you for a month."

"Let's go with option C, which is neither. But gee, thanks for the vote of confidence."

"I'd be sad if you were kidnapped, if that helps."

Justin paced the length of the camper. "It doesn't."

"That hurts, J. Anyway, what's up? You've been teaching bull riding at the rodeo school for a few weeks. How's that going?"

"Good. It doesn't eat up my entire day. The rest of my time is spent dealing with rough stock and livestock."

"Better you than me. But seriously, I can tell you're agitated so let's skip the bullshit and tell me what's wrong."

His brother knew him well. He stopped pacing and took a deep breath. "I'm in trouble, Jack. Big time."

"Spill it."

"I'm in love."

A pause, then, "Love? You fell in love in a month?"

"It's been almost two months. I kept it to myself because I wasn't sure at first if it was the real deal, given my shitty track record."

"And now?"

"I know it's real. And yeah, I know how it sounds." Justin heard a feminine voice in the background. "Is Keely there?"

"She says she doesn't care how it sounds. She wants to know how it *feels*."

"Amazing. And scary as fuck."

The call was disconnected. Then five seconds later his phone buzzed with a FaceTime request from Keely. Justin sat on the edge of the small couch and answered.

Keely's beautiful face un-pixilated and she grinned at him. "Hey, bro. I figured this would be easier so Jack and I can both be in on this monumental event and you'll only have to explain it once. Hang on until Jack gets in here." The camera jiggled and then Jack's and Keely's heads were side by side. "Okay. Ready."

Justin squinted at the bedframe on the wall behind them. He'd stayed there enough times he recognized it. "Why are you guys in the guest bedroom at your house?"

"We were um…checking something out in here when you called," Keely said with a smirk.

Right. Jack had probably been checking out his wife's ass and then he pounced on her.

"We bought a new mattress and Keely lured me in here to test it out," Jack said smugly.

"TMI, much, GQ?" Keely said, elbowing him.

"Where are the kids?" Justin asked.

"Mom has them overnight."

Justin's eyebrows went up. "All four of those hellions at one time? That's kinda mean."

Jack rolled his eyes. "Mom loves it. Now quit stalling. Out with this love thing."

They stared at him expectantly and Keely added, "What's her name?"

"Callie. She works at Grade A. She also bartends in town. We've been spending every moment we can together and she just…gets me in a way no woman ever has."

"What's she like?"

"Beautiful, sexy, funny, sweet and thoughtful."

Keely sent him a soft smile while Jack's gaze turned shrewd. "If she gets you then she's aware of the entire picture, not just the small vignette?"

Typical Jack, using a twenty-dollar word when a fifty-cent one would do. "Have I told her I've built up a decent nest egg? Nope. I think that, more than anything, would spook her. She's had a rough go all her life, so she's awful damn independent."

"You sound proud of that."

"I am. If you knew what she'd gone through…" He shook his head. "Anyway, there's one other thing. It was an issue for me at first, but after bein' with her awhile, I don't even think about it anymore. It'll bother some people, but that ain't my problem. I—"

"Justin," Keely said sharply in her mom voice, "stop beating around the bush and tell us."

"Callie is twenty-two," he blurted out.

His brother and sister-in-law shared a look. Then they burst out laughing. He might've heard Keely singing Taylor Swift's "Twenty-two" between gut-busting guffaws, which caused Jack to laugh harder.

Christ. Were these two high? This was not the reaction he'd expected.

At least they weren't lecturing him. Or warning him.

Finally their laughter tapered off and Justin said coolly, "You done?"

"Oh, lighten up, cradle robber," Jack said with a grin.

Justin groaned. His brother would tease him about this for-fucking-ever.

"I have a couple of questions," Keely said with that prepared-to-get-grilled gleam in her eyes. "How long did you fight yourself on this before you accepted you loved her and the age difference didn't matter?"

"Longer than I should have." He looked away and confessed, "But I needed to get my head straight that she and I weren't in the same place at that age. I was a cocky, judgmental, know-it-all punk at twenty-two. I knew how to work hard, but that doesn't mean I actually worked hard. I lived hard. Did a lot of dumb shit. Made mistakes that hurt other people…" He gave Keely a sheepish smile. They'd dated for a time before Keely ended up with his brother and he'd acted like a whiny prick over it, even when he'd dumped her, even when he knew in his gut that Jack was the better man for Keely in every way that counted.

"Water under the bridge," Keely said softly. "We've all been cocky, know-it-all assholes at some point in our life. It happens at different times for different people. Some people are never like that, and some people never grow out of it." Smirking, she pointed at her husband.

"You'll pay for that later, buttercup," Jack said haughtily and did something out of camera range that caused Keely to yelp.

Justin had always envied their relationship, the ease and the tease between them, the way they'd accepted each other and hadn't tried to change one another. The fierce way they fought because they loved fiercely too. And to think he'd found that with Callie made him want to shout it from the freakin' rooftops.

"Were you afraid to tell us because you thought we'd judge you for her age?" Keely asked. "Because I'll remind you, dumbass, that my best friend married my oldest brother. He's thirteen years older than her, and they were meant for each other. Period."

"Or did you worry we'd try and convince you that it couldn't be real love because it happened so fast?" Jack asked.

He shrugged. "Like I said, I had to work it out myself before I took the next step with her. And it annoyed the fuck out of me that she just let me be her friend. We worked together, saw each other every damn day for weeks and she treated me the same as she always had. Drove me fuckin' crazy. She didn't pull any of the stupid tryin' to make me jealous type of crap that I would've done at her age had the situations been reversed."

"And that's when you knew she was the one?" Keely said dreamily.

"No. I realized that when my truck broke down and she thought I didn't have enough money to fix it, so she just handed over all her tips from that week." Justin swallowed hard—Christ, that still got to him. "We weren't even together and she cared enough about me to help me out, even when I knew that deep down, she was still hurting from me pulling away from her."

"Omigod, that is so sweet! She sounds like a doll."

That's when the camper door slammed and Callie barreled inside, fuming. "Do you know what that motherfucker Disanto just asked me? If I'd mind dropping his shirts off at the drycleaners since I have to go into town anyway. Can you believe the balls on that prick? I reminded him that I work for the Gradskys, not him and he'd better stop assuming that employees in the maintenance department give two hot shits about makin' his life easier." She made an aggravated sound. "I wanted to knock him off his damn high horse, but he'd probably break a nail or something since he's such a fucking pussy and then I'd get in trouble for it." She flopped down next to him. "Sorry. I'm feeling extra stabby today."

Yeah...maybe *doll* wasn't the best term to describe his Callie. Although she'd give "Bride of Chucky" a run for her money.

But Justin grinned. God, he adored this woman. Slipping his arm around her shoulders, he tugged her into camera range. "C'mere, sweetness, and meet my family."

"What? Jesus Christ, are you on FaceTime? You couldn't have let me know that before I—"

He kissed her to shut her up. "But your tangents are so damn entertaining and you were on a roll, Calamity."

She groaned and dropped her forehead to his shoulder.

"Look at the screen, darlin'."

She lifted her head and waved. "Hey. I'm Callie. Nice to meet you."

Both Jack and Keely were grinning.

Then Callie gasped and touched Keely's face onscreen. "Hey, I remember you! You were super nice to me at Carter's wedding. And how is it that you look exactly the same and it's been like...seventeen years?"

"You have my permission to marry her," Keely joked. Then she squinted at the screen. "Wait. Callie? As in...Callie Morgan?"

"Yep. Small world, isn't it?"

"Very," Jack said smoothly. "We're coming through there in a few weeks so we can meet you in person."

Why was this the first he'd heard of it? And why did that sound like a threat to Callie? Because that protective big brother shit wasn't gonna fly with him, especially when he was a forty-year-old man who knew his own damn mind. Then Justin's eyes narrowed on his brother, taking in the totally faked innocent look on Jack's face. The fucker was having way too much fun with this.

"I hope it's soon enough that Justin will still be around."

"It's sort of ironic that I'm seeing my nephew Kyler next week," Keely said. "You remember him?"

"The ringbearer from the wedding?" Callie paused. "Vaguely. I mostly remember the kid had a death grip on my hand during the ceremony and followed me around the entire night."

"For years he swore he was gonna marry you," Keely said with a sly grin at Justin. "It was cute."

"Aw, that is cute. Tell him I said hey."

"And tell him that Callie's with me now," Justin said with a snarl.

"And...that's our cue to go," Jack said. "Good talking with you, Justin. Nice meeting you, Callie. See you soon."

The screen went blank.

"Are you mad?"

Justin faced her. "Keely is a shit-stirrer. She knew I'd be jealous and get pissy about Kyler—"

Callie put her fingers over his lips. "Not at her. Mad at me for barreling in here and probably coming off like a crazy woman to your family."

"God, no. You came home from work and blew off steam." Justin ran his knuckles down her jawline. "You never have to worry that I'll expect you to be any way except the way you are. I won't apologize for it and neither should you."

"Justin."

"C'mere and kiss me."

Callie crawled onto his lap and fused her mouth to his, holding his face between her palms. Kissing him sweetly. Kissing him hungrily. Kissing him like she couldn't get enough of him.

He latched onto her ass, encouraging her to grind against his cock that was getting harder by the second.

But she pulled away and scooted off his lap, grabbing his hands and tugging him to his feet.

"We takin' this into the bedroom?" he said huskily.

"Nope. Put your hands on the ceiling."

He opened his mouth to ask why, but she shook her head. "Just do it."

Callie stood in front of him and began to unbutton his shirt. Kissing his chest as she revealed each bit of skin, stopping only when his shirt hung open completely. She emitted a soft purring sound as she ran her hands across his collarbones, over his pecs, around his ribs. Then she used the tips of her fingers to trace his abs and the line of light hair that disappeared into the waistband of his jeans.

God, he loved how she touched him. Sometimes she used her nails. Sometimes she used her teeth. Sometimes she dragged her silken, sweet-smelling hair across his skin, no contact except that light tickle that drove him out of his fucking mind. But no matter which way she touched him, roughly or softly, she wore a look of possession, and that alone was enough to make him come undone.

She nuzzled the patch of hair on his chest as she undid his belt. Then that sassy little tongue lightly outlined the ridge of muscle that separated his chest from his sternum as she unbuttoned his jeans.

Justin couldn't stop the hissing sound of need that passed through his lips when Callie's hot breath flowed across his nipple. Then she started to suck on the tight disk with deep, suctioning pulls that he felt in his balls.

The woman rocked at multitasking. As she toyed with his nipples until he was goddamned shaking like a junkie, she eased the zipper down on his jeans and stroked his cock. His fully erect cock that jumped against her hand begging for more, demanding she wrap her fingers around and start the stroking, pulling, tugging that would drive him to spurt all over her hand.

Callie lifted her head from his chest and smirked. "Stop groaning like you're gonna die. I'm getting there."

Do not say not fast enough, *or she will walk the fuck outta here and leave you hanging. You* know *this about her, you know she does things on her own time frame, and you want her doing you.*

Justin ground his teeth together and said nothing.

She whispered, "Good boy" and slid her hands to his hips, hooking her fingers into his boxers and jeans and yanking them to his knees.

Sweat snaked down his spine and gathered on his forehead, but no way was he moving. Hell, he was barely fucking breathing as Callie lowered to her knees.

He locked his legs to keep himself from toppling over.

This was his favorite part. Her soft little sigh of happiness right before she took his cock in her mouth. She did it every time, and every time, he fell harder for her. Not just because she worshipped his cock like a porn star, but because she truly loved giving him pleasure as much as she loved getting it from him.

"Callie."

"Huh-uh," she said as she flattened her tongue against the weeping tip of his cock. "Who am I?"

"Calliope. Christ, you're killin' me."

"Say it again."

"Calliope. Please." Justin called her by different names during the day, sweet and funny terms of endearment, but she'd asked him when they were stripped bare in body and soul, to call her Calliope, a name she rarely used, but the one name she wanted to belong only to him.

Big, tough, life experienced man that he was, he'd nearly wept like a fucking baby when she'd made that simple request.

Then she swallowed him to the root and his brain short-circuited.

The primal need for release turned him into a grunting, groaning animal, incapable of communication beyond, "Oh yeah...please...fuck...more...Christ...harder, baby...fuck me."

She stayed with him, focused on him, as he pumped his hips into her face.

Abs tight, fists clenched, ass locked, he came in a long groan of ecstasy and she swallowed him down, the muscles in the back of her throat milking him until he had nothing left.

As the ultimate relaxation loosened every part of him, he felt Callie smile against his thigh after he'd slipped out of her mouth.

He managed a soft "What?" through his labored breathing.

"I love your cock."

"I love you."

He felt her tense up.

"Justin—"

"I mean it, Calliope. I love you. I've loved you since you made me figure it out on my own that I loved you enough to fight myself for you." He dropped his arm and curled his hand around her face, forcing her to look at him. "Not great timing, telling you that after a blowjob, but baby girl, it ain't my dick that's talkin' right now. It's me. And I'm telling you that I love you."

Did his Callie burst into happy tears and confess she loved him too? No.

She lifted an eyebrow and said, "You're sure it's not your dick talking?"

He outlined her bottom lip with the pad of his thumb. "Sweetness, you put him in a coma, he's incapable of talkin' right now."

She laughed and poked his rapidly softening cock. "Okay. I believe you."

Justin waited, silently willing her to say it back.

But Callie rolled to her feet and sent him a look that was almost...shy.

"Talk to me. Have I freaked you out?"

"A little. But I don't run when I get freaked out like some people do."

He blushed. Jesus. Would he ever not feel like an idiot for bailing on her like that?

"So here's the deal. I'll return the sentiment, in the same way."

"Meaning...you'll blurt out how you feel about me after I've gone down on you?"

"Yep. Fair is fair." She placed her hand over his heart. "But the truth is...I feel the same way. I've been waiting for the right time to tell you, too."

Despite his jeans hobbling him, despite the fact his goddamned heart was about to bust out of his chest, Justin dropped to his knees in front of her and yanked her pants down. "Brace yourself, darlin'. This is gonna be the fastest I ever get you off."

Chapter Ten

Story of her life…one step forward and two steps back.

Callie received the acceptance letter to Stacey James Institute three months after she'd become a Colorado resident.

As an incoming student, she'd applied for a butt-load of grants, scholarships, and loans. Those had come through and she'd been awarded enough money to pay for the first year of the two-year program.

The email she'd received yesterday indicated a "backlog" for the student housing options, meaning all the housing they'd contracted to offer students at a reduced rate was full.

At first she'd thought no big deal, she could live in her camper. But the school was south of Denver and there weren't many campgrounds in the area that accepted longer term permits. With the legalization of cannabis, there'd been an increase in the number of homeless people, and the few campgrounds in the Denver area capped the length of time to stay in a calendar year at two months. No exceptions.

The closest campground without restrictions was a forty-five minute drive through metro Denver closer to the mountains. For Denver having a decent public transport system, neither the buses nor the light rail went that far out. And in reading the fine print, Callie saw that the hookup facilities were closed from November through April anyway.

So she'd looked into leasing a lot in a trailer court. But again, the lots were full and most of them had a waiting list of a year or more. And the lot rental was four times more than she'd expected it'd be, which was a double whammy because the trailer courts were mostly in the worst parts of Denver.

Now, she had less than two weeks to come up with a solution.

Callie closed the lid on her laptop.

Two weeks. Hard to fathom that her life would be completely different two weeks from now. She'd be in classes Monday through Friday, with every other Saturday being optional to shadow professionals in their job settings, allowing students to gauge their interest on adding accreditation for becoming a nail tech, makeup artist, or an esthetician. That would give her two full weekends off every month. She'd never had that option. What would she do with herself? Given the rent situation, she'd probably have to get a job.

Maybe she could skip the line, so to speak, in continuing to work within The Sly Fox franchise in the metro area. She'd given her notice last week, and the Barbarian had been surprising cool about Callie moving on. She hadn't even penalized her by cutting her hours. She'd miss her coworkers. Their mutual promises of keeping in touch...nice in theory, but the reality of the bar business was people came and went all the time and losing track of them was more the norm than sustaining a lifelong relationship.

And speaking of relationships...Callie had no idea what the future held for her and Justin, or if they even had a future. She loved him like crazy and he told her he loved her too, showed it to her in every way that mattered—not just in bed.

He'd moved in with her the day after they'd burned up the sheets for the first time. Living with him had been much easier than living with her mom and her sisters, probably because he didn't have a lot of stuff. Callie had gotten used to crawling into bed next to him after her shift at the bar. He never complained that she woke him up, not even when he had to be up at the crack of dawn. He just sleepily gathered her into his arms and asked how her night had gone. Bonus points for her man that she'd never caught him snoring during the retelling of the events of her shift. Part of her suspected his curiosity stemmed from whether any male customers had gotten handsy with her. In the interest of keeping her job, and keeping Justin's blood pressure down, they agreed that he limit his visits to the bar to once a week for a maximum of two hours.

She knew he loved watching her dance—he just hated that other men got to see her move like that too. On the nights he came to watch her, she gave him an over-the-top show. A different routine than he'd ever seen. They rarely got out of the parking lot before Justin was on her, in her, owning her, whispering in explicit detail exactly what'd raced through his deliciously dirty mind as he'd watched her dancing for him. Then they'd go at it again when they returned home.

He'd taken her sexual education to a whole new level. Sometimes he'd love her so tenderly, so reverently, tears sparked from the pure joy of their intimate connection. Other times, the bossy cowboy appeared, ropes in hand to tie her to the bed, or to the chair, teasing her until she literally screamed. The cocky man really loved when their campsite neighbors/coworkers gave him a high five the next morning after joking about rockin' the camper. He sure didn't have a problem with her age then. The man was so proud she couldn't even be mad at him.

Callie would miss all of the couple things they shared that she'd never had. Their inside jokes. Cooking together in their little love nest. Arguing at the grocery store when he went over their allotted budget because he'd bought her flowers. Working the pens together. The quiet moments when she rested her head on his chest and just listened to him breathe.

She'd done pretty well convincing herself that she respected him for making her no promises and for believing hers that this was just sex without strings. Despite knowing her last image of him would be his tail lights and the mud flaps on his truck as he drove away, she'd gone into this relationship with her eyes and her heart wide open.

Most days she'd convinced herself that realizing she was capable of such love and passion was enough. That the memories of him and falling for him would be enough.

Today wasn't one of those days.

The rodeo school session ended next week. Justin hadn't mentioned his plans for after that and Callie wondered if he knew where he'd end up. It'd stung to learn that he'd been offered the instructor's position for next session at Grade A Rodeo Academy—gossip she'd heard from Deke and Lana, not from her man himself.

Maybe he'd decided to make it a surprise for her.

Maybe he hadn't told her because he didn't want the pressure from her to take the job when he didn't want it.

During the hours they'd spent hanging out at the bonfire with their friends and coworkers, Justin shared a million stories of his life on the road. While she loved hearing about that part of his life, she'd hated it too because she recognized the longing in his voice went deeper than melancholy. It was an innate part of him and she'd never ask him to walk away from it. And Justin understood how important school was to her, so he wouldn't ask her to give up her dream to be with him wherever the road took him. So they were at an impasse.

Callie closed her eyes, trying to calm her chaotic thoughts and focus on the positive.

He showed you that you're worthy of love.

He accepted every part of you.

He treated you with respect.

He was proud to be with you.

He made you laugh.

He made you swoon.

He made you his with every touch, every breath, every look, every moment you spent together...and how in the hell are you ever gonna live without him?

Her tears fell. This time, no amount of telling herself that life would go on and she could just suck it up and deal would make them stop.

That's how Justin found her, sobbing hysterically with her head down on the table, tears soaking her laptop.

"Callie?"

She snuffled and warned herself to get it together.

"Sweetness, are you hurt? Are you sick?" His normally gentle hands frantically tried to push her hair away from face. "Baby girl, look at me."

She shook her head.

"Talk to me."

She shook her head again.

Then Justin merely plucked her up and carried her to the couch, settling her on his lap so she couldn't hide.

The concern in those beautiful green eyes did her in. More stupid tears fell. She managed to stutter, "I'm s-s-s-sorry."

"For what?"

"For c-c-c-crying like a b-b-baby."

Justin clamped his hands on either side of her head. "Are you hurt?"

Yes, it feels like my heart is being ripped from my body and my soul has been shredded, but no biggie.

"Callie," he said sharply, "are you hurt?"

"No."

"Thank you, Jesus."

She stared at him, greedily drinking in every nuance of his face, the faced she loved so much, the face she'd never get tired of looking at. The laugh lines by his eyes. The frown lines by his mouth. The scowl line between his eyebrows. The smooth, tan skin that indicated a life spent out in the elements. The tightness flattening his full lips. The hard set of his chiseled jawline. The softness in his green eyes. How many more times would she be this close to him?

"You're scarin' the life outta me with the way you're eyeballin' me like you ain't ever gonna see me again."

Callie wasn't surprised he'd picked up on that. His intuition was unparalleled when it came to her.

"What's wrong?"

"I got notice from the housing department today. Basically there's no room at the inn. Everything is a go for me to start school, but I don't have a place to live. I can't find a spot to park my camper. So I have no choice but to start checking Craigslist to find a room to rent and it's overwhelming." Tears shimmered in her eyes again. "Nothing ever works out for me the way I want it to. I've always been able to suck it up and move on from disappointment, but it's been harder this time."

His gaze turned shrewd.

And Callie was as intuitive when it came to his emotions. She knew he wanted to say, "All them tears for that little bitty worry, don't seem like you" because he'd seen her cry one time in the months they'd been together.

Instead, he said, "Sounds to me like you've already got a plan in place."

Why didn't he sound happy about that? "I'm trying to get it handled."

"By yourself. Just like you always do, huh?" His thumb gently stroked her cheekbone.

"It's what I do, Justin. I've always had to rely on myself." He knew that. He'd told her that was one of his favorite things about her, so why did he seem so unhappy about it now?

"Did you ever think maybe you oughta talk to me and I could help you figure something out?"

Her chin shot up with defiance. "You've got your own stuff to deal with. You don't need to be burdened with mine."

Then he was nose-to-nose with her. "Not a goddamned thing about you is a burden to me, Callie. Not. One. Damn. Thing. Don't you know that by now?"

She shook her head.

"Then, baby girl, it's time I showed you." He settled his mouth over hers, his tongue pushing between her lips to get inside, as if he needed a taste of her to survive. The kiss wasn't the ravenous, teeth-knocking one she'd expected, but a sweet outpouring of love that pushed her tears to the surface again.

He released her mouth and rested his forehead to hers. "Do you trust me?"

"Yes." Then Callie took the biggest chance of her life and said, "I love you, Justin Donohue. No matter what happens in the next two weeks, I'll always love you with everything I have, with everything I am." She managed a smile. "Granted, I don't have much."

Justin said nothing. He pressed his lips to hers, gifting her with a lingering kiss.

Then he lightly slapped her ass. "Grab your purse and get your boots on. We're goin' for a ride. I wanna show you something."

* * * *

When Justin said "ride" Callie assumed he'd take her to the corral, saddle up the horses and they'd hit the trail for a few hours to take her mind off her troubles because being outdoors with him always worked.

But he'd meant a ride in his truck straight into the heart of Denver.

He'd been quiet during the drive. Not necessarily brooding, but Callie knew he had something on his mind. Her emotional exhaustion overtook her and she rested her head on the console between their seats.

Justin smoothed his hand over the top of her head and down her hair, petting her in the way that made her feel spoiled...and very sleepy.

She woke up to the sounds of honking horns.

After she'd shaken off the cobwebs, she looked around. "Why are we in a concrete bunker?"

He laughed. "It's a parking garage." He whipped around the corner and chose a spot with a warning sign above it:

PRIVATE PARKING ONLY—VIOLATORS WILL BE TOWED

"Uh, I think you'd better park somewhere else."

"Nah. It's okay." He grinned. "I know the owner. Come on, let's go."

Justin clasped her hand and led her into the elevator. He punched in a code and they started to ascend.

He wasn't talking, in fact, he seemed nervous, so Callie choked back the million questions on the tip of her tongue.

She watched the lighted panel and saw they'd reached the seventeenth floor. The doors opened and a sea of burgundy carpet spread out, as if they were on the executive level of some fancy hotel.

This was too bizarre. She tugged his hand. When he stopped and faced her, she crowded him against the wall. Well, crowded was optimistic because the solidly muscular and singularly stubborn man wouldn't budge unless he wanted to. "Where are we? Some fancy-schmancy hotel?"

"No. But would you hate that?" He touched her face. "Me takin' you someplace swanky? Letting room service bring us food because we were too exhausted from fucking in a big, soft bed and a gigantic whirlpool tub to leave the room?"

Callie set her hand on his chest. "I wouldn't hate it, but you know I don't need that from you either."

"I know." He pointed to the door across from them with a number on it. "This isn't a hotel. It's an apartment building."

Okay. That was even stranger.

Justin kept his hold on her hand until they reached the end of the hallway. He sorted through his keys and shoved one in the lock. A green light flashed. Then he led her inside.

Callie stopped in the middle of the living room. Not that it looked lived in, with one long couch, a gigantic TV, and a coffee table. She turned and saw a large kitchen, open concept, with an eat-in breakfast bar that spanned the length of the marble countertop. The bank of windows snagged her attention next and she wandered over to look across the city of Denver and to the mountains in the distance. She turned back around to see Justin's fine butt parked against the back of the sofa. His arms were crossed over his chest.

"I'll admit you've stumped me, cowboy hottie. What is this place?"

His eyes searched her face. "My apartment."

She started to say something smart, but she noticed the tense set to his shoulders. Actually, his whole body was rigid. The man was wound tight as she'd ever seen him. "Your apartment," she repeated.

"Yeah. I haven't been here much in the past. So this place will solve your housing problem. You can live here while you go to school."

Callie's eyes nearly bugged out of her head. "What do you mean live here? There's no way I can afford a place like this, Justin. No way." That's when it occurred to her that Justin shouldn't be able to afford it either. She pinned him with a look.

He smiled at her. "I see you've done the math."

"What is going on? Who are you?"

"Baby girl, you know who I am straight down to the bone. You're one of the few who do." He patted the spot beside him. "Have a seat."

"I'll stand. Start talking."

"It's a long story."

"I doubt that. Boil it down to the basics for me."

He grinned at her again. "God, I love your sassy mouth."

Callie shook her finger at him. "Save the sweet words. Give me the facts."

"I did pretty well in the PBR. Better than most as far as not blowin' all the money I earned because my brother Jack wouldn't let me. He taught me a few things about investing money, I taught myself a few things and I…" Justin stood and rubbed the back of his neck. "I was smart enough after the second go-around not to let myself be used by women who only wanted me for what I could buy them."

"You have money?" Callie said finally.

"Yeah."

"So you're not a broke-down cowboy, living hand to mouth? Restless and on the road searching for your next job?"

Justin looked at her and shook his head.

Her mind raced. "Why would you let people think that of you?"

"Because I'd had enough of women and former friends thinking of me as a damn meal ticket. A free ride. I'd earned the money. But the greedy women that I thought loved me felt entitled to spend it. When I wised up and said no more, I learned that my money and fame had more appeal than who I was out of the arena and the spotlight." He paused. "It was a hard lesson that I shoulda learned a lot faster than I did. But when I did wise up, I also felt broken down. I had no direction in my life so I just…rambled. Did what interested me. Spent time with my family. Helped out friends who'd stuck by me in good times and bad, and darlin', I can count them on one hand."

Callie balled her hands into fists and tried to be calm, but her anger won out. "So when you were so self-righteous and accused me of lying to you about my age, you were lying to me about…this? Is it because you thought I was some kind of gold digger too?" Then she had another lightbulb moment. "That's why you spent five fucking weeks as my friend. You were judging my character?"

Then Justin was right there, his strong hands curled around her biceps. "The fact I didn't disclose that I wasn't hurtin' financially had nothin' to do with you. I've been livin' that mindset for so goddamned long that some days it shocks the crap outta me to realize that I don't gotta muck stalls to earn a paycheck."

She tried to squirm out of his hold. "How nice for you that you have so many options!"

"Callie—"

"Did you have a good laugh when I gave you money to fix your truck?" Her body went hot with shame. To think that it'd made her proud that she could help someone else out for a change.

"No. That one sweet, selfless act made me realize I was in love with you."

"Why should I believe you?"

He froze.

She blinked at him, trying her damndest not to cry.

"Because it's the truth. I fell in love with you then and every day I love you more. Do you hear me?" He shook her a little. "I. Love. You. You're the first woman who's ever loved me for *me*, not for what I could give them. You loved me even when you knew that's probably all I could give you. Just my love. And I knew part of you didn't want to love me because you believed it wouldn't matter and I'd leave you anyway. That I'd hop in my truck at the end of the session and not look back. But you still took a chance on loving me with that big heart of yours, didn't you? You gave me all of you and you accepted every part of me, even my goddamned age. It didn't matter because you love me. I *know* you do."

Had he said that to convince himself? Or to remind her?

"It's been killin' me the last couple of weeks, watchin' you struggle against askin' me to stay with you. I knew that even if the thought of me leavin' you broke your beautiful heart into a million pieces, that you'd let me go. Like you said you would. Because you're a woman of your word, right?"

Callie managed to nod.

"You'd let me go because you're used to disappointment. But that ends right now."

"Justin—"

"I'm not letting you go without a fight. I've waited a long goddamned time for you, Callie. You're mine in a way that makes me so fucking proud. Not just because you're young and sexy and beautiful. But because you're strong-minded, soft-hearted, resilient, and hopeful. Despite the shit hand that life dealt you, you always find the good, the funny, and the ironic in every situation. You saw all of that in *me* when I no longer saw it myself. Money can't buy that. You gave that optimism back to me, freely, and from your heart. You make me happy in a way I never thought I'd deserve. And baby girl, I know I make you happy too. I *know* it," he repeated. "And it also makes me so fucking proud that I can do that for you. That you *let* me do that for you." He paused. "Remember when you told me that you didn't believe in all that soul mate, romantic bullshit? Because you'd never seen it or experienced it?" Those green eyes of his went soft. "Maybe that's why you're fighting me on this. Because you don't recognize that's what this is between us, Callie."

Stunned by his admission, she just stared at him.

"You deserve all the happiness in the world and I'm making it a personal life goal to give it to you every day."

She found her voice. "What are you saying?"

"You've never had anyone take care of you. From here on out, that's gonna change. I'm takin' care of you. That doesn't mean controlling you or making your decisions. That means you'll move in here, with me, while you're going to school."

When she started to ask a question, he shook his head.

"I'm not done. You proved to me that you don't care about the age difference between us. So use that same logic and apply it to the financial differences between us. Prove to me you don't care."

Callie got a tiny bit annoyed that he was using her own damn argument against her. "How?"

"I know you'd have a problem letting me take care of you as my girlfriend. I'm hoping that you wouldn't have that same mindset as my wife." Justin dropped to one knee.

Omigod, omigod, omigod, what was he doing?

"I'd planned to do this in a more romantic setting, but it's more important that you know now that I'm not messin' around with this. I'm not waiting. I love you. You are the best thing in my world. I want to spend every day of my life with you by my side and every night with you in our bed, in our home. So, Calliope Jane Morgan, will you marry me?"

His chest was heaving. His eyes were hot. He was the most magnificent male she'd ever seen. And he was hers. All hers. All she had to do was say the word. One word to have everything she ever wanted.

"Yes."

Maybe she shouldn't have laughed when he stood up so fast his knee creaked.

But he laughed right along with her. "You sure you want me, creaky parts and all, sweetness?"

Nodding, Callie framed his face in her hands, staring at this beautiful man she loved so much, grateful that she'd get to look at him, be with him for years to come.

"I know I'm a little old to be thinking about startin' a family, but if you want that, a few years down the road after you've established yourself in your career, well...I'd be happy to knock you up a time or two."

She kissed him, her heart so full she couldn't speak.

But as usual, Justin knew everything she was saying and feeling. He swooped her into his arms and carried her into his bedroom, ready as always to let their bodies do the talking.

* * * *

Later, Callie was splayed across his flannel sheets, thoroughly spent. Her stomach grumbled but she didn't have the desire to move even an inch away from her fiancé.

Fiancé. What a trip.

They hadn't made wedding plans or talked logistics of merging their lives together permanently. They'd just celebrated their new permanence in their own fun, naughty way.

Justin gave her back a long sweeping caress, from the nape of her neck to her butt. "I'm already slacking on my duties as your husband-to-be by letting you go hungry." He kissed her shoulder. "We can order in pizza, or I can sneak over to my mom's apartment and see what she's got for food."

Callie lifted her head. "Your mom's apartment?"

"Yeah. Jack and Keely have an apartment here too. We sorta took over this end of the building."

"Why? None of you live here full-time, do you?"

"Nope. When we sold the farm, we knew we were giving up more than just work and land. It'd always been our home. A place for our family to gather. Jack and Keely built Mom her own place on their acreage in Wyoming, and she can do her own thing, but she's close to them and her grandkids. Jack's always had an apartment in this building and I bought one because he swore it was a good deal. When two other apartments came up for sale on this floor a few years back, we bought them. Mom has one and since Jack and Keely have so many kids now, they had to expand into more space. So even when I couldn't get to Wyoming for Christmas or Thanksgiving, we could all meet here."

"I love that. I can't wait to be a part of it." She'd immediately clicked with her soon-to-be sister-in-law last week when Keely and Jack and their kids had stopped by the rodeo school for a few hours. Callie had only met Justin's mom via FaceTime, but she seemed like a sweet lady. It hadn't crossed Callie's mind that Justin's mother was the same age as her grandmother until he'd pointed it out.

Callie hadn't told her mom and sisters much about Justin. They tended to be cynical about men—especially cowboys—and she'd wanted to enjoy her time with Justin without their judgment. But now she couldn't wait to introduce them to the man who owned her, body and soul.

"Whatcha thinking about?" he said after he kissed her shoulder.

She looked at him curiously. "You won't mind living here full-time?"

"I love Denver. It's a great place to be based out of, for…whatever I decide to do next."

"Well, Richie Rich, it's not like you've gotta find a job next week to pay your cell phone bill this month."

He pinched her ass and she yelped. "I love that you're already rolling with this."

"Oh, I'm sure I'll have issues with it. Not in a bad way, more like…*Fine, cowboy hottie, you can pay for dinner.* But I do foresee the…*No, big spender, I do not need another Land Rover* conversations too."

He laughed. "I'm gonna have so much fun spoiling you, Callie."

"Because I don't want it?"

"No, because you don't expect it. That'll make it ten times more fun for me." Justin rolled her onto her back and positioned himself above her. "Speaking of fun…"

"I thought you were gonna feed me?"

"After," he murmured against her neck and he began to kiss his way down her body.

"Are you always gonna be this insatiable?"

Justin lifted his head and grinned at her. "Yep. Will that be a problem?"

"Nope." She shoved his head back down. "Now get to work."

"This is the job I was meant to do."

"Making me orgasm several times a day?"

His eyes were serious when he said, "Takin' care of you."

"Sweet talker," she said huskily. "The pay isn't great."

"Then it's a good thing I'm not in it for the money."

Epilogue

Two years later...

"Callie! Woman, get a move on. We're gonna be late." Justin fiddled with his bolo tie. Why wouldn't this damn thing lay flat?

"Cool your jets, cowboy. I doubt they'll start my graduation party without me."

Justin looked up and wished he hadn't.

Jesus, his wife looked hot. Like fuck-me-now hot in that slinky dress the same amazing blue as her eyes. Although calling it a dress was a stretch as the damn thing barely covered her sexy little ass. But the cut of the dress—and those black stilettos—did spectacular things for her killer legs. Not to mention the sparkly top half of the dress, with a well-placed cutout, showed her mouth-watering cleavage. The fabric cupped her tits, ribs, and hips so tightly that his hands got a little twitchy with jealousy.

Finally his gaze moved to her face. Callie still had the ability to render him speechless. She'd gone all out with her makeup and hair tonight, which was perfect advertising for the skills she'd learned over the past two years. As the top student in her class, she had her pick of the best salons in Denver. He assumed she'd choose one the first day, because she had a work ethic that flat-out amazed him and claimed she was ready to earn her keep.

As if. He kept his woman very well, thank you very much.

But to his surprise, Callie insisted on taking two weeks after graduation to really consider her options since this was the start of her career and not just a job.

While they both loved living in Denver, they'd spent a lot of time in Wyoming with Jack, Keely, and their brood, as well as his mom. Callie's sisters were off at different colleges and she didn't see them as often as she liked. She'd cajoled her mom into taking a few vacation days so they could hang out in the big city. Callie had even convinced her mom to let her do a full makeover on her—hair, makeup, clothes. Mary was thrilled to look ten years younger, but her real thrill was seeing her daughter in her element, doing what she'd always dreamed of, and her pride that Callie had gotten there on her own.

As glam as Callie could make any woman look, including herself, she remained a country girl at heart. She loved the outdoors and hanging out with family and friends. When they were ready to start their own family in a couple of years, and when she was ready to open her own salon, he hoped she'd consider moving to Sundance.

That'd be ideal for him and Jack, since they'd gone into business together last year and started a nonprofit.

That'd also be ideal for Keely and the ten billion other McKay women, since they begged Callie every time she came to town to do their hair and makeup—and paid her well for her expertise.

"You're staring. Is this too much?" Callie asked.

"No, sweetness, you're breathtaking. I couldn't talk for a moment."

She smirked. "And yet you still manage to be a sweet talker."

Justin set his hat on the side table and ambled toward her.

Callie immediately backed up. "Get that look out of your eyes, buddy. It's your fault we're running late the way it is."

"My fault? Baby girl, I don't believe those were cries of pain an hour ago when I was on my knees in the shower with you." Most days he felt like a horny twenty-year-old kid when he saw his wife naked. Or clothed. He couldn't keep his hands off her.

"Whatever. I'm finally all put together and you are not going to tear me apart."

"Can I muss you up…just a little?"

Her eyes heated and he was tempted to do a fist pump. But she realized she was giving in and held her hand out. "Nope. Tonight is the one night I can't have a single hair out of place."

"Our friends and family are already impressed with you. And I'm proud as hell of you for all the hard work you've put in for the past two years. It's paid off. You finally get to live your dream."

Callie sauntered forward and wreathed her arms around his neck.

Then she planted those blood red lips right on his. "I've been living the dream from the moment I met you. This is just...icing."

"So that means you love me, huh?"

"Yep." She kissed him again. "But you still can't muss me up."

Dammit.

On her way to pick up her coat, she gave him the fuck-me look that she had the first night in the bar. "But I'll let you tear me apart any way you want when we get home."

* * * *

Also from 1001 Dark Nights and Lorelei James, discover Roped In, Stripped Down, Strung Up, and Tripped Out.

Sign up for the 1001 Dark Nights Newsletter
and be entered to win a Tiffany Key necklace.

There's a contest every month!

Go to www.1001DarkNights.com to subscribe.

As a bonus, all subscribers will receive a free copy of
Discovery Bundle Three
Featuring stories by
Sidney Bristol, Darcy Burke, T. Gephart
Stacey Kennedy, Adriana Locke
JB Salsbury, and Erika Wilde

Discover 1001 Dark Nights Collection Five

Go to www.1001DarkNights.com for more information.

BLAZE ERUPTING by Rebecca Zanetti
Scorpius Syndrome/A Brigade Novella

ROUGH RIDE by Kristen Ashley
A Chaos Novella

HAWKYN by Larissa Ione
A Demonica Underworld Novella

RIDE DIRTY by Laura Kaye
A Raven Riders Novella

ROME'S CHANCE by Joanna Wylde
A Reapers MC Novella

THE MARRIAGE ARRANGEMENT by Jennifer Probst
A Marriage to a Billionaire Novella

SURRENDER by Elisabeth Naughton
A House of Sin Novella

INKED NIGHT by Carrie Ann Ryan
A Montgomery Ink Novella

ENVY by Rachel Van Dyken
An Eagle Elite Novella

PROTECTED by Lexi Blake
A Masters and Mercenaries Novella

THE PRINCE by Jennifer L. Armentrout
A Wicked Novella

PLEASE ME by J. Kenner
A Stark Ever After Novella

WOUND TIGHT by Lorelei James
A Rough Riders/Blacktop Cowboys Novella®

STRONG by Kylie Scott
A Stage Dive Novella

DRAGON NIGHT by Donna Grant
A Dark Kings Novella

TEMPTING BROOKE by Kristen Proby
A Big Sky Novella

HAUNTED BE THE HOLIDAYS by Heather Graham
A Krewe of Hunters Novella

CONTROL by K. Bromberg
An Everyday Heroes Novella

HUNKY HEARTBREAKER by Kendall Ryan
A Whiskey Kisses Novella

THE DARKEST CAPTIVE by Gena Showalter
A Lords of the Underworld Novella

Discover 1001 Dark Nights Collection One

Go to www.1001DarkNights.com for more information.

FOREVER WICKED by Shayla Black
CRIMSON TWILIGHT by Heather Graham
CAPTURED IN SURRENDER by Liliana Hart
SILENT BITE: A SCANGUARDS WEDDING by Tina Folsom
DUNGEON GAMES by Lexi Blake
AZAGOTH by Larissa Ione
NEED YOU NOW by Lisa Renee Jones
SHOW ME, BABY by Cherise Sinclair
ROPED IN by Lorelei James
TEMPTED BY MIDNIGHT by Lara Adrian
THE FLAME by Christopher Rice
CARESS OF DARKNESS by Julie Kenner

Also from 1001 Dark Nights

TAME ME by J. Kenner

Discover 1001 Dark Nights Collection Two

Go to www.1001DarkNights.com for more information.

WICKED WOLF by Carrie Ann Ryan
WHEN IRISH EYES ARE HAUNTING by Heather Graham
EASY WITH YOU by Kristen Proby
MASTER OF FREEDOM by Cherise Sinclair
CARESS OF PLEASURE by Julie Kenner
ADORED by Lexi Blake
HADES by Larissa Ione
RAVAGED by Elisabeth Naughton
DREAM OF YOU by Jennifer L. Armentrout
STRIPPED DOWN by Lorelei James
RAGE/KILLIAN by Alexandra Ivy/Laura Wright
DRAGON KING by Donna Grant
PURE WICKED by Shayla Black
HARD AS STEEL by Laura Kaye
STROKE OF MIDNIGHT by Lara Adrian
ALL HALLOWS EVE by Heather Graham
KISS THE FLAME by Christopher Rice
DARING HER LOVE by Melissa Foster
TEASED by Rebecca Zanetti
THE PROMISE OF SURRENDER by Liliana Hart

Also from 1001 Dark Nights

THE SURRENDER GATE By Christopher Rice
SERVICING THE TARGET By Cherise Sinclair

Discover 1001 Dark Nights Collection Three

Go to www.1001DarkNights.com for more information.

HIDDEN INK by Carrie Ann Ryan
BLOOD ON THE BAYOU by Heather Graham
SEARCHING FOR MINE by Jennifer Probst
DANCE OF DESIRE by Christopher Rice
ROUGH RHYTHM by Tessa Bailey
DEVOTED by Lexi Blake
Z by Larissa Ione
FALLING UNDER YOU by Laurelin Paige
EASY FOR KEEPS by Kristen Proby
UNCHAINED by Elisabeth Naughton
HARD TO SERVE by Laura Kaye
DRAGON FEVER by Donna Grant
KAYDEN/SIMON by Alexandra Ivy/Laura Wright
STRUNG UP by Lorelei James
MIDNIGHT UNTAMED by Lara Adrian
TRICKED by Rebecca Zanetti
DIRTY WICKED by Shayla Black
THE ONLY ONE by Lauren Blakely
SWEET SURRENDER by Liliana Hart

Discover 1001 Dark Nights Collection Four

Go to www.1001DarkNights.com for more information.

ROCK CHICK REAWAKENING by Kristen Ashley
ADORING INK by Carrie Ann Ryan
SWEET RIVALRY by K. Bromberg
SHADE'S LADY by Joanna Wylde
RAZR by Larissa Ione
ARRANGED by Lexi Blake
TANGLED by Rebecca Zanetti
HOLD ME by J. Kenner
SOMEHOW, SOME WAY by Jennifer Probst
TOO CLOSE TO CALL by Tessa Bailey
HUNTED by Elisabeth Naughton
EYES ON YOU by Laura Kaye
BLADE by Alexandra Ivy/Laura Wright
DRAGON BURN by Donna Grant
TRIPPED OUT by Lorelei James
STUD FINDER by Lauren Blakely
MIDNIGHT UNLEASHED by Lara Adrian
HALLOW BE THE HAUNT by Heather Graham
DIRTY FILTHY FIX by Laurelin Paige
THE BED MATE by Kendall Ryan
PRINCE ROMAN by CD Reiss
NO RESERVATIONS by Kristen Proby
DAWN OF SURRENDER by Liliana Hart

Also from 1001 Dark Nights

TEMPT ME by J. Kenner

About Lorelei James

Lorelei James is the *New York Times* and *USA Today* bestselling author of contemporary erotic romances in the Rough Riders, Blacktop Cowboys, Mastered, Rough Riders Legacy and Need You series. She also writes dark, gritty mysteries under the name Lori Armstrong and her books have won the Shamus Award and the Willa Cather Literary Award. She lives in western South Dakota.

Connect with Lorelei in the following places:

Website
Facebook
Twitter
Instagram
Facebook Reader Discussion Group
Newsletter

Discover More Lorelei James

Roped In: A Blacktop Cowboys® Novella

Ambition has always been his biggest downfall...until he meets her.

World champion bulldogger Sutton Grant works hard on the road, but his quiet charm has earned the nickname "The Saint" because he's never been the love 'em and leave 'em type with the ladies. When he's sidelined by an injury, he needs help keeping his horse in competition shape, but he fears trying to sweet-talk premier horse trainer London Gradsky is a losing proposition--because the woman sorta despises him.

London is humiliated when her boyfriend dumps her for a rodeo queen. What makes the situation worse? She's forced to see the lovebirds on the rodeo circuit every weekend. In an attempt to save face, London agrees to assist the notoriously mild, but ruggedly handsome Sutton Grant with his horse training problem on one condition: Sutton has to pretend to be her new boyfriend.

But make believe doesn't last long between the sassy cowgirl and the laid-back bulldogger. When the attraction between them ignites, London learns that sexy Sutton is no Saint when that bedroom door closes; he's the red-hot lover she's always dreamed of.

The more time they spend together, the more Sutton realizes he wouldn't mind being roped and tied to the rough and tumble cowgirl for real...

* * * *

Stripped Down: A Blacktop Cowboys® Novella

Never challenge a cowboy to a little naughty competition...

A flirty game of sexual truth or dare between best man, Wynton Grant, and maid of honor, Melissa Lockhart during their BFF's wedding reception results in a steamy hookup.

But their plans for a *one and done* change when a family crisis leaves Wyn shorthanded at the Grant Ranch. Experienced horsewoman Mel volunteers to help out and gets way more than she bargained for living under the same roof as the sexy rancher. Playing house has never appealed to Wyn...until now.

But the feisty redhead is keeping secrets and Wyn's not above stripping her bare—body and soul—to get to the bottom of it...

* * * *

Strung Up: A Blacktop Cowboys® Novella

Rancher Creston Grant retreats from the world after he loses the love of his life... Can his former flame, rodeo cowboy Breck Christianson prove he's a changed man who can give Cres a second chance at love?

* * * *

Tripped Out
A Blacktop Cowboys® Novella

Where there's smoke...

Stirling Gradsky abandoned the corporate rat race for a more laidback lifestyle. So it's ironic she's stuck working with a hard-bodied, know-it-all scientist who treats her like a stoner instead of a stone cold business woman capable of running a large scale cannabis operation. Dr. Hot and Tattooed with the big...brain needs to stop sampling their product; he's under the half-baked idea that he's the boss.

Dr. Liam Argent's doctorate isn't in chemistry, but from the moment he meets his sexy new coworker, there's enough heat between them to short out all the lights in the grow house. First item on his agenda? Clearing up the sassy, blunt blonde's hazy notion that she's in charge.

Sparks fly as their attraction blazes. But can they weed out their differences without getting burned?

Racked and Stacked

Blacktop Cowboys® Book 9
By Lorelei James
Now Available

Opposites don't just attract in the West–they sizzle–and Wyoming has never been hotter than in the latest sexy Blacktop Cowboys® novel from the *New York Times* bestselling author of *Hang Tough*.

Growing up with three older brothers, Larissa "Riss" Thorpe defines the term tomboy–a moniker that never mattered to her until she crossed paths with sexy cowboy playboy, Ike Palmer. His declaration that he prefers his women soft and feminine is the one benefit to becoming his business partner. Since Riss is obviously not his type, there's little chance they'll mix business and pleasure when they're in close quarters on the road together.

Former cattle broker Ike Palmer was ready for a new chapter in his life when he partnered with Riss, a contrary redhead who lords her mechanical abilities over him at every turn. Ike raised his three younger sisters; he knows a thing or three about how women work. The problem is…Riss is unlike any woman he's ever met.

With the odds stacked against them, Riss and Ike will have to choose between the stubbornness that keeps them apart and the fiery attraction that could lead to something more…

* * * *

Normally Riss wore baggy and stained coveralls, or painter's pants, paired with an equally baggy hoodie.

But she had cleaned up very well for this wedding. She'd tried to tame her crazy red curls into a ponytail. Leaving her neck exposed accentuated the ivory tone of her skin. She'd used eyeliner that made the green hue of her eyes even more arresting—the color ranging between pale green and peridot, depending on her mood. Her emerald-colored bridesmaid's dress molded to her, reminding him—and every other male—that she'd been blessed with a truly magnificent body, especially her tits.

"Why are you staring at me?" she demanded. "It's sure takin' you a long damn time to come up with an insult."

"Truce, remember?" Ike allowed his gaze to encompass her face, as if he was truly seeing her for the first time. "You don't look awkward, Riss. You look really pretty." Before he could stop himself, he ran the back of his knuckles down her cheek, from her temple to the tip of her chin. "It pains me—"

"To admit that?"

"No. And stop interrupting me. It's a pain to see that you covered up your freckles."

She blinked at him. "Why?"

He shrugged. "I like them. They're just...you." *That sounded like a come-on.* He backtracked. "Besides, makeup hides your level of anger so I can't see your face getting red."

"Then that means you can't see me blushing either."

"Why would you be blushing?"

She blushed even deeper. "Because you said I looked pretty."

He barely kept his jaw from dropping. This woman could babble about blow jobs in public without batting an eye, but a compliment brought heat to her cheeks? He didn't know what the hell to even say to that.

"Genuine flattery from Palmer the Charmer is enough to make any woman swoon."

She did a shimmy-shake with her shoulders—was that supposed to convey a swoon?—sending her enormous breasts swaying, and Ike's avid gaze tracked every shift of flesh against fabric. "At least you were looking at my face." Another shimmy-shake sent her breasts bouncing. "Not that you are now. It's hard to look away from the girls when they're out of captivity, isn't it?"

Jesus. "How long do we have to stick around after the newlyweds are allowed to leave for real?"

Surprisingly, she didn't needle him about the rapid subject change. "I'm not sure. I know Jade's mom and dad are staying until the last guest leaves. I thought the Mud Lilies would be whoopin' it up tonight and chase everyone away, but they've been on their best behavior."

"I suspect Jade demanded obedience from them the same as she did from you."

"Me obedient? Never. My toned-down behavior is strictly voluntary."

Ike preferred wild Riss. She had a spontaneity he lacked. "Like that's a shocker."

"I am shocked that none of the Mud Lilies have stalked you and demanded a dance."

"Me too. I figured since they were behaving they'd track me down and regale me with stories about the wild bachelorette party you threw," Ike said.

Riss rolled her eyes. "You really think that Garnet would let anyone else plan a night of debauchery for her only granddaughter? She barely let me host a bridal shower for her."

"That's strange, ain't it?"

"You don't know the half of it. Garnet's cronies have called dibs on throwing Jade a killer bachelorette party."

"They do understand that a bachelorette party is supposed to take place *before* the wedding, right?"

"Not in the Mud Lilies' universe. According to Jade, the only way Tobin would agree to let them plan a party was if it took place *after* the wedding and the honeymoon."

His eyebrows rose. "Tobin is usually putty for them old gals."

"Not when he overheard Garnet and Miz Maybelle discussing the 'ultimate Vegas girls' weekend,' which included a trip to a gun range, a skyscraper zipline challenge and an overnight stay at the Desert Dreams Dude Ranch. He forbade them from taking Jade out of Wyoming. Not fun for him to fly to Vegas to bail them all outta jail."

"Luckily for him the law around here is very familiar with the ladies' shenanigans," he said with a laugh.

"And so are the bail bondsmen. I'm pretty sure Tobin believes the Mud Lilies will forget about it and move on to something else."

"I hope so. I hate Vegas."

Riss tipped her head back and looked at him. "Seriously? Why?"

"Besides the fact I don't gamble?"

"Dude. There's lots to do in Vegas besides gamble." She studied him. "Isn't Vegas a stock contractor's dream? Standing on the podium at the national finals in December? Aren't the national finals an annual destination for all the folks who put on rodeos across the country? I'd think you'd be jumping at the chance to do a meet and greet there. Especially since Hugh is based not more than four hours away in Cali, right?"

She'd totally busted him. Now he had to backtrack. "Hugh couldn't get meetings with the event coordinators he'd been in touch with throughout the year. So we opted not to and decided to push harder for meetings next year, after we've got a few successful events under our belts." Ike shifted to face her. "Will you be bummed if you don't end up in Sin City for a belated bachelorette party?"

"Yes. And no. I mean, most people have that 'what happens in Vegas' mind-set only when they're on the Strip. I prefer to put half-truths into everyday life." She laughed at his alarmed expression. "You don't do that?"

"Do what?"

"Mess with people? Strangers mostly, but sometimes even friends?"

"Explain 'mess with,' Thorpe."

"Say you're out of town and you're in a C-store to feed your craving for Funyuns, Reese's peanut butter cups and Fanta grape soda. You're in line to check out, and the woman behind you says, 'Bad breakup?' So instead of telling her to mind her own business, you complain good-naturedly that you wish, but the truth is your wife is pregnant with twins and she gets ridiculous cravings late at night. That you're glad not to be buying something super weird like last time, when she craved stewed tomatoes and Three Musketeers and ate them together."

Ike couldn't believe how fast Riss had whipped up that story.

She poked him in the chest. "See? Even you're intrigued about that weird-ass craving. So the Nosy Nelly who began the conversation will either ignore you from that point on, or she'll start telling you about what she craved during pregnancy."

"And if I run into Nosy Nelly again?" he prompted.

"You won't."

"So you just flat-out lie to people?"

"I prefer to call it creating an altered reality."

"In other words…you lie." Ike leaned closer and caught a whiff of Riss's coconut perfume. How in the hell wasn't he supposed to imagine oiled-up bodies in tiny bikinis when that damned tropic aroma teased him?

She poked him in the chest again. "Oh, lose the judgmental look. You used to be a salesman—a *professional* creator of alternate reality, whereas I'm merely an amateur."

He couldn't pull off indignant so he laughed. "Have you ever created an altered reality with me?"

"Besides this whole 'truce' thing? No. Are we messing with our friends by not telling them about our truce? Absolutely."

"Is that how you ended up with the big Johnson? Created an altered reality and he bought into it?"

Riss groaned. "I wish. That's a perfect example of why I should always veer away from using my real name."

"I don't want to know how many times you've created an alternate reality, do I?"

"Probably not. But you could tell me the most spontaneous thing you've ever done." She tugged on his tie. "Bonus points if it's a dirty sexual scenario."

"No judgment?"

"None."

"Coming up with the idea of buying out Renner Jackson and taking over JSC," he said in a rush, not having the guts to add that it was the worst idea he'd ever followed through on.

"Interesting." She toyed with the ends of his bolo tie. "Your answer is business related and it hasn't been about business between us for months."

He chucked her under the chin until her gaze collided with his. "I wish I had done something spontaneous and cool in my life to wow you with, Riss."

"It's not too late." Her vivid green eyes issued a challenge. "The next time you have a chance to act out or act up...don't hesitate. Be impulsive."

"And if I don't have the balls to follow through with it, then I should lie my ass off to you anyway?"

Riss smirked. "Now you're getting it, Palmer."

On behalf of 1001 Dark Nights,

Liz Berry and M.J. Rose would like to thank ~

Steve Berry
Doug Scofield
Kim Guidroz
Jillian Stein
InkSlinger PR
Dan Slater
Asha Hossain
Chris Graham
Fedora Chen
Kasi Alexander
Jessica Johns
Dylan Stockton
Richard Blake
and Simon Lipskar

89879347R00090

Made in the USA
San Bernardino, CA
03 October 2018